"Sit back down," he com[...] dropped into his cha[...] beer."

She made a face at him. "W[...] much fun to be with?"

He gazed up at her through those fine dark eyes. She wanted to bend across the iron table between them and kiss that sexy mouth again, to have those big, muscular arms of his wrapping tight around her.

"Please." He said the word a little roughly. But kind of earnestly, too. Like he really, truly wanted her to stay.

When, exactly, did she become such a complete pushover for this man? The night of the tequila? Maybe.

More likely, it had started long before that, when he was always coming into the Sea Breeze and sitting at the bar, keeping her company while she worked. He would nurse a beer or two, maybe have sliders or fish tacos and fries. When things weren't too busy, they would talk. He was a good listener. Too serious, maybe. But the thing about Dante was he really did care—how a friend was doing, if everything was all right.

She sat down and picked up her half-finished beer. "Bad day?"

* * *

THE BRAVOS OF VALENTINE BAY: They're finding love—and having babies!—in the Pacific Northwest

Dear Reader,

I love those stories where opposites not only attract, but end up discovering they're just right for each other. They fill each other's empty spaces, make each other...more.

Bartender and soon-to-be history teacher Grace Bravo is twenty-three, happily single, open-minded, freethinking and a bit of a wild child. Due to a shortage of funds caused by unwise investments in the creative and scientific endeavors of previous boyfriends, Grace is also still living in the home of the big brother who raised her. She wants nothing as much as to get out on her own.

Dante Santangelo, a detective sergeant with the local police force, is thirty-two and divorced, a dedicated dad to his eight-year-old twin daughters. He's a good man, a man you can count on, down-to-earth, traditional in his outlook on life and absolutely positive he'll never get married again.

Grace and Dante are friends. They enjoy each other's company in a casual way. There's nothing romantic going on between them—until one warm summer night that changes everything...

Dante has a lot to learn about love, and Gracie is just the one to school him but good. I hope you find their story as much fun to read as it was for me to write and that *Their Secret Summer Family* leaves you secure in the knowledge that love is the answer, even for a guy who isn't all that sure of the question.

Happy reading, everyone,

Christine

Their Secret Summer Family

CHRISTINE RIMMER

HARLEQUIN
SPECIAL
EDITION

HARLEQUIN®

**SPECIAL
EDITION™**

Recycling programs
for this product may
not exist in your area.

ISBN-13: 978-1-335-89453-3

Their Secret Summer Family

Copyright © 2020 by Christine Rimmer

This edition published by arrangement with Harlequin Books S.A.

For questions and comments about the quality of this book,
please contact us at CustomerService@Harlequin.com.

Harlequin Enterprises ULC
22 Adelaide St. West, 40th Floor
Toronto, Ontario M5H 4E3, Canada
www.Harlequin.com

Printed in U.S.A.

Christine Rimmer came to her profession the long way around. She tried everything from acting to teaching to telephone sales. Now she's finally found work that suits her perfectly. She insists she never had a problem keeping a job—she was merely gaining "life experience" for her future as a novelist. Christine lives with her family in Oregon. Visit her at christinerimmer.com.

Books by Christine Rimmer

Harlequin Special Edition

The Bravos of Valentine Bay

The Nanny's Double Trouble
Almost a Bravo
Same Time, Next Christmas
Switched at Birth
A Husband She Couldn't Forget
The Right Reason to Marry

The Bravos of Justice Creek

James Bravo's Shotgun Bride
Ms. Bravo and the Boss
A Bravo for Christmas
The Lawman's Convenient Bride
Garrett Bravo's Runaway Bride
Married Till Christmas

Montana Mavericks: Six Brides for Six Brothers

Her Favorite Maverick

Montana Mavericks: The Lonelyhearts Ranch

A Maverick to (Re)Marry

Visit the Author Profile page
at Harlequin.com for more titles.

For Gaye McGill, in honor of her
golden retriever–German shepherd mix, Flip,
who was the inspiration for the hero's dog, Owen,
in this story. Gaye would like readers to know that
Flip was the best of the best
and Gaye misses her greatly.

Chapter One

Grace Bravo was going too fast and she knew it.

But she really needed to cheer herself up. And it was a beautiful, sunny first day of June on the Oregon coast, the perfect kind of day to drive with the windows down, playing "Shut Up and Drive" really loud. The fir-scented air blew in and swirled around her, stirring her hair as she bopped right along with Rihanna. She was beating out rhythm on the steering wheel and swinging around curves with abandon.

Too bad she wasn't really feeling it—not the beauty of her home state, not the sunshiny day, not the warm summer air whipping her hair around her face, not even the hard-driving beat of the music turned all the way up.

And then the light bar started flashing behind her. A siren blared.

"No!" she cried. "This cannot be happening..."

But it was. Grace turned off the radio and took her foot off the gas. Easing her eight-year-old RAV4 to the side of the road, she put it in Park and switched off the engine. The white Valentine Bay police cruiser, lights still flashing, pulled in behind her, the nerve-shredding siren cutting off in midshriek.

A ticket was definitely in her future.

She shouldn't be the least surprised. It was all just more crap piled on top of an already craptastic day.

Thinking dark thoughts, she raked her windtangled hair back off her forehead and watched in her side mirror as the officer—tall, dark haired, broad shouldered, tanned and very fit, in Valentine Bay PD blues and black wrapback sunglasses— emerged from the cruiser.

It took her a second or two to realize who he was.

Dante Santangelo?

No way.

Grace had known Dante forever. His only sister

was married to one of her brothers. Once or twice a week, he dropped by the Sea Breeze where she worked. They got along great, Grace and Dante. She'd always considered him a friend.

Until now, anyway.

"Are you kidding me?" she muttered sourly when he leaned in her window.

"Gracie, you were speeding," he chided—like he was really sorry, but being sorry wouldn't stop him from doing his job. He took off those black sunglasses and gave her a melty look as his plush mouth curved in a warm smile. "License and registration?"

"This is so wrong," she grumbled.

He just kept on leaning in the window, those velvety, coffee-brown eyes patient, like he could wait forever for her to stop being grumpy and pass him her papers.

"Fine." She leaned across the console, popped open the glove box, got out her registration, handed it over, then fished her wallet from her bag and gave him her license, too.

"Thanks," he said. "I'll be right back…"

"I was afraid you'd say that."

He turned for his cruiser. With a groan of frustration, she flopped her head against the seat and closed her eyes.

He was back in no time with a clipboard. "Here you go." He handed her documents through the window.

She took them. "Thanks," she sneered, and couldn't resist reminding him, "I give you the good beer. I don't even let you tip me." Actually, he always tipped her, anyway. But she always meant it when she told him not to.

Did he chuckle as he wrote on his clipboard? Sure sounded like it to her. One big shoulder lifted in an easy shrug. "And I'm giving you the good ticket."

"That makes no sense. There is no good ticket." And yeah, it was a stretch, but she might as well try her feminine wiles on him. Tossing her messy hair a little, gazing up at him with sad, wide eyes, she pleaded pitifully, "Do you *have* to?" He just kept writing out the ticket. "It's been a bad day," she whined. With feeling. "And now *this*."

He passed the clipboard in the window and handed her his pen. "Initial here and here. And then sign here."

"A hundred and sixty bucks? You can't be serious."

He said nothing, just continued to look at her with that thoroughly annoying expression of gentle patience on his handsome face.

She huffed out an exasperated sigh, took her sweet time reading the whole damn thing and did what he told her to do, giving back the clipboard and pen when she was done.

He passed her the ticket and launched into a little spiel about the deadline to respond and how to contest the citation. When he finally shut up about it, he leaned in the window again. "Okay, that's out of the way. Now. Are you all right?" His expression had morphed from patience to real concern.

She glared at him, just to drill it home that she would be a lot better if he hadn't pulled her over. "Not really."

"You need someone to talk to?"

Share her problems with Dante? The idea never would have occurred to her. Yeah, she considered him a friend. But not a cry-on-your-shoulder sort of friend. She'd known him her whole life, practically. And she'd always considered him hot and all, with those smoldery good looks and that broad, hard body.

But he was nine years older, thirty-two to her twenty-three. He'd been married and divorced and he had twin daughters. The guy was a settled, responsible sort of man who would no doubt consider her flaky and immature if she griped about her fight with her bossy eldest brother and whined over her paltry bank balance, which was keeping her from getting her own place.

And about her miniscule bank balance? That was all on her. She'd inherited a little money back when she turned eighteen. If she hadn't enjoyed spending it so much, she would have plenty of money to move.

She should thank Dante for offering to listen to her problems, insist that she was fine, say she would see him the next time he stopped by the bar—and then wave goodbye.

But the thing was, his offer kind of gave her the warm fuzzies. Dante was a tough guy. He didn't let many people close. That he seemed to really want to be there for her made her feel better about herself, somehow.

"You'll be sorry," she warned and waited for him to back out.

But he didn't back out. "I get off at five. I'll see you at the Sea Breeze."

"No, you won't."

"Why not?"

"I can't cry on your shoulder at my place of work. That would be totally unprofessional—and besides, I'm off tonight." She was pretty sure that would do it. He would tell her to drive carefully and turn for the cruiser.

Didn't happen. "How about my place, then?"

Dante's house. She hadn't been there in years—not since she was sixteen and babysat his twins that one time when his then-wife, Marjorie, couldn't get her regular sitter. "You don't have to do this, you know?"

"Hey, come on. What's a friend for?" He upped his offer. "I'll open a bottle of wine."

She waved the ticket at him. "After this, you owe me a nice bottle of tequila. I'll bring the tacos."

He didn't even blink. "Six o'clock?"

For the first time since he'd pulled her over, she gave him a smile. "I'll be there."

Dante had a really nice house—a shingled, rambling, ranch-style place on an acre of wooded land overlooking the ocean. He'd bought it about a decade ago, in the midst of the last housing crisis, when a house like Dante's went for half what it was worth now.

Grace admired the pretty setting as she carried bags of take-out tacos up to his front door. On three sides, the house was surrounded by trees. In back, it overlooked the ocean.

Dante, in worn jeans and a gray crewneck T-shirt that showcased his muscular arms, pulled the door open before she rang the bell. "Right on time. And you brought the tacos, too—here." He took the bags from her. A friendly-looking dog bumped around him, tail wagging. Dante gently warned, "Owen, play nice." The dog had short floppy ears, a sweet face and a red-brown coat with a blaze of white at the throat. His paws were white, too.

She greeted him. "Hello, Owen." With an eager whine, the dog sat and gazed up at her hopefully. "Part golden retriever, right?" she asked Dante.

He nodded. "Golden and German shepherd."

"He's very handsome." She knelt to scratch his thick ruff, glancing up as she let Owen lick her face. "You get the good tequila?"

"Come on inside." He stepped back and ushered her in. "You can see for yourself." He led her to the kitchen area, which was open to the living space, with concrete tile counters and glass backsplashes.

"The counters are beautiful," she said.

"Thanks. I like to change stuff up now and then."

Back when she was sixteen and the pinch-hit babysitter, the counters were white tile—and right now, the bottle of tequila was waiting on the island. She picked it up. "Anejo." The word meant "smooth" or "restful." Tequila Anejo had to be aged in oak barrels that did not exceed six hundred liters for at least a year. "Thank you."

He gave her a nod and gestured at the limes in the wire basket nearby. "You want to shoot it?"

"Have you met me? I'm a purist."

"Perils of being a bartender, huh?"

"That's right. You develop definite opinions when it comes to enjoying good liquor." Actually, bartending was an interim job for her while she'd waited for a teaching job to open up locally.

She had a degree in history with a minor in education from Reed College and she'd recently snagged her dream job. This fall, she would be teaching history at Valentine Bay High. In the meantime, she was still working at the bar, sometimes days and sometimes nights. She liked the flexible schedule.

Dante took a couple of stemless wineglasses from a cupboard. "Will these do?"

"Perfect."

They decided to sit out on the deck and enjoy the view. She helped him carry everything outside, including a pitcher of ice water, which made her laugh. It was so Dante, to make sure they stayed hydrated while they were getting blasted.

It was gorgeous outside and wouldn't be dark for hours. The deck faced a stretch of wooded yard. Farther out, twisted, windblown evergreens framed the edge of the cliff and the top of a narrow trail leading down to a nice stretch of beach below. Off in the distance, the ocean gleamed, pearly blue to the horizon.

Grace sat in a cushioned deck chair at a cast iron table beneath the shade of a big white umbrella. At Dante's insistence, she drank a tall glass of water and ate two tacos before settling back to sip tequila. Owen had stretched out at her feet.

"Okay, I gotta admit." She tapped Dante's glass with hers. "*This* is the life—how are the girls?"

Dante took a slow sip. It went down smooth and hot.

It was nice, really, sitting out here with Gracie. He'd always liked her. She was fun and easy to be with.

And she'd grown up to be gorgeous, with all that silvery blond hair, those soft lips the rich pink color of the inside of a conch shell and those sapphire-blue eyes. Her skin was so pale. She looked like she might bruise from a touch—not that he'd ever make a move on her or anything. They had a way-too-complex history.

Her third-born brother, Connor, had been Dante's best friend all their growing-up years.

But then Connor had broken the bro code. He'd fallen in love with Dante's sister, Aly, and married her. Dante had barely forgiven Connor for that, when Connor divorced Aly for reasons that really weren't reasons at all. Dante had sworn never to speak to the jackass again.

Then last year, Aly and Connor had gotten back together. They'd married each other for the second time last October and Aly had given birth to their daughter, Emelia, just last month. Dante and Connor were friends again now.

And really, Dante had always thought of Gracie Bravo as a kid.

Well, until lately, anyway. Today, she wore faded denim shorts and a cropped top. Following her out here from the kitchen, he couldn't help staring at her ass and her strong, pretty legs, at all that gorgeous, delicate skin…

"Dante. Helloooo." Laughing, she reached across the table and lightly batted his arm. "Nicole and Natalie? How are they doing?"

"Good. Real good." He ordered his dirty mind off Gracie's ass and back to the much safer subject of his twin daughters. They were eight now. They mostly lived with his ex-wife, Marjorie, in Portland, where they went to school. He had them every other weekend and for seven weeks in the summer.

Gracie asked, "When do they come for vacation?"

"A week from this coming Saturday."

"You're counting the days."

He tipped his glass at her. "I always do." He was a family man, through and through. His ex-wife was a good mother. Still, he just felt better when his girls were with him.

Gracie asked, "So how's it going with the new stepdad?"

At Easter, Marjorie had married Dr. Roger Hoffenhower. Roger was a family psychologist and a really nice guy with a big heart. "Terrific." He drank more tequila.

Gracie scoffed. "Smile when you say that."

"I like Roger." He set his glass on the table and turned it slowly. It was almost empty. Against his own better judgment, he added, "I also kind of hate Roger."

"Why?"

He put the glass to his lips again, sipped the last of the golden liquid inside and then slowly swallowed. "Roger is an open wound of feelings and sensitivity." In other words, pretty much everything Dante wasn't. "Plus, Nic and Nat like Roger. A lot. Can you blame me for hating the poor guy?"

She gave a husky little laugh that he found way too attractive. "I think anything I say right now will probably be wrong."

"Smart girl—and why are we talking about Roger, anyway?"

"Er, because you like him—but you hate him, which means you're conflicted about Roger and that's not only interesting, it's the kind of thing you need to talk about with a friend."

He stared at her, unblinking. "But we're not here to talk about Roger."

"You started it. Officer." Those sapphire eyes twinkled at him.

"You're the one who asked about Roger."

"But then you told me how you really feel about the guy. That's my cue to encourage you to tell me more."

"Wrong." He raised his glass to her. "We're risking liver damage for your sake, remember? You need to tell me all about what's bothering you so I can take a crack at saying all the helpful stuff that will make you feel better."

"Clearly, you are at least as sensitive as Roger."

He grunted. "Don't bet on it. But I'm here and willing to listen."

She picked up the bottle and poured them both more tequila. They sat back, just sipping, for a few peaceful minutes. It was nice, he thought. Companionable.

She was staring off toward the ocean when she said, "I had a fight with Daniel this morning." Daniel Bravo was the eldest of the Bravo siblings and something of a father figure to all of them. When their parents died years ago on a trip overseas, Daniel had gotten custody of them and raised them to adulthood in the house where they grew up. "It was a stupid fight and we both apologized after. Daniel and I used to get into it all the time, but it's been better lately. Truly. We get along really well now, as a rule. But I'm sick of living in the house I grew up in and frankly, my big brother is sick of having me there, though he would never admit it..."

They both continued sipping the excellent tequila as Gracie rambled on, looking way too cute and kind of sad, too, explaining about the small trust fund she and her siblings had each inherited from their lost parents. She went on to explain about her trips to Europe in the summers while she was in college, about the writer she lived with one summer. And the sculptor the next and the inventor the year after that.

"That was in Italy, the inventor," she said. "His name was Paolo and he invented things that had a tendency to explode."

Mostly, she explained, she supported these guys with her inheritance while she was with them. "You have to understand, Dante. They were brilliant and interesting. It was England and Ireland and Italy. Best of all, Daniel wasn't there to call me foolish and wasteful and taken advantage of by irresponsible guys. I had the time of my life."

"But…?"

She rolled those big blue eyes. "But Niall and Keegan and Paolo were expensive. And that means that by the end of that third summer, I was kinda, sorta broke."

"How broke?"

She plunked her glass down and poured herself another. He probably should have suggested they put the brakes on the drinking. But he was enjoying himself. That was the thing about Gracie. He'd discovered in the nights he'd hung out at the Sea Breeze with her that she was not only easy on the eyes, she was funny and smart—with a lot of heart.

Gracie Bravo was the whole package, really. He felt better about life in general somehow, when he was hanging around her. He held out his glass and she gave him more, too.

"There's good news, though," she said, after she'd put the bottle down and sipped again from her glass.

"Tell me."

She raised her glass high, as though saluting the trees and the cliff and the whole damn Pacific Ocean. "My perfect job has finally opened up at Valentine Bay High. I'll be teaching world history in the fall."

"Congratulations. That's terrific." He tapped her glass with his.

"Thank you. Also, I've been budgeting responsibly for the last two years, saving what money I can. By Christmas, I'll have enough to get my own place."

So what was the problem? "Okay, then. You had a fight with Daniel, but you already patched that up."

"Yeah."

"And you've got your money situation under control."

"I do. It's true."

"That doesn't sound so bad."

Her forehead got scrunchy as she considered what he'd said. "You don't get it. Dante, I need my own space *now*, I really do. Daniel and Keely are good to me." Keely was Daniel's second wife.

His first wife had died shortly after giving birth to twins—a boy and a girl—almost four years ago. "And the house is really big, I know. But still, they've got the twins and now Marie." Marie was Daniel and Keely's daughter—and about a year and a half old now, if Dante remembered right.

Gracie drank more tequila. Dante did, too.

"Keely and Daniel have a right to their own house," Gracie said. "And I want a life without my big brother breathing down my neck. I want that life now. My BFFs Carrie and Erin are already roomies—with no room for me. I could move in with Harper and Hailey." They were two of her sisters. "They've got that rambling old cottage Aislinn owns." Her sister Aislinn had married recently and moved to a ranch owned by her new husband. "But Harper and Hailey are like a team, you know? I always feel like a fifth wheel around them. So anyway, I thought I had an interim solution to the problem, a room in the house of a nice older woman named Sonja Kozlov down on Cherry Street. But then, early this afternoon, Sonja gives me a call. Her son has moved home unexpectedly and my interim space is no longer available. She gave me back my first, last and deposit and that's that. I'm still living in my brother's house. Probably till Christmas."

The good news was, he actually had a solution to her problem. "You want the cabin? It's yours."

"What cabin?" Squinting, she craned across the table toward him. "Are you drunk?"

He gestured toward the thick copse of trees behind her, on the south end of his property. "I have a guest cabin, I guess you could call it. Over there. See the trail going into the trees?"

She turned and stared where he pointed. "Wait. I see it. A log cabin, green tin roof?"

"That's it. It's one room—and a bathroom. Nothing fancy, but it has everything you need. Power, basic appliances. Running hot and cold water. A woodstove for heat if you need it. I even had Wi-Fi hooked up in there last year when one of the station house dispatchers needed a place to stay for a few months."

"How come you don't just rent it out on a regular basis?"

He shook his head. "I don't want some stranger living a hundred feet from my back deck. Luckily, you're no stranger. You can have it for as long as you want it, free of charge."

She sat back in her chair. "That's not right."

"Sure, it is."

"I can pay you what I would've paid Sonja, at least."

He put up a hand. "Stop. Let me do this for you. Like you said, you need a place of your own and the cabin is just sitting there empty."

She slapped the tabletop. "Wait."

"What?"

"We should discuss this tomorrow when we're both sober."

"Oh, come on, Gracie. I solve your problem for you and you can't just say thanks, I would love to stay in your log cabin for free?"

"Nope. Not tonight. Tonight is for tequila and commiseration." She let out a heavy sigh. "Right now, we need to get on to a more interesting topic. Let's commiserate about love."

"That does it."

"Huh?"

He grabbed the bottle and moved it to his side of the table. "No more tequila for you."

"You're such a hard-ass, Dante—but I still intend to talk about love."

He helped himself to another glass. After all, the bottle was in his control now. Might as well take full advantage. "Go right ahead."

She'd slipped off her pink sneakers and was giving a very happy Owen a tummy massage with her toes. "I love your dog."

Owen knew she was talking about him. With a gleeful little whine, he rolled over and got up.

"Come on, sweetheart," she coaxed.

With a sigh of pure contentment, Owen put his head across those amazing white thighs of hers. She petted him, stroking down his back, scratching him behind the ears. Owen shut his eyes and basked in the attention.

She asked, "Does he just stay home alone when you're working?"

He explained about the nice lady named Adele who lived on the next property over. "Adele runs a sort of doggy daycare, but it's casual. She's there all the time. I can drop Owen off and pick him up pretty much anytime that suits me. When I work nights, he stays here, but I can always manage to get home sometime midshift to check on him, give him a little attention and a short walk outside."

She made a humming sound low in her throat and petted the dog some more. Dante began to hope that maybe they'd left the subject of love behind.

But then she sat back in the chair and stared up at the sky. "Where were we? Right. Love. I can't say for sure that I've ever really been in love." A long sigh escaped her. "But I have been infatuated, like head over heels, you know? Sadly, I always

go for the brilliant ones, the ones nobody understands, the emotional fixer-uppers, I suppose you
could say." She slanted him a quick glance. "You
know about fixer-uppers, don't you?"

He did like watching those pink lips move. "Explain it to me."

"Fixer-uppers are expensive. I've blown my wad
on fixer-uppers." She let out a giggle, and then got
serious again. "So right now, I can't afford another
relationship—and could you maybe not look so
completely disapproving?"

He blinked. "I'm not." Was he?

"Yeah, you are. You're reminding me a little
of Daniel. Talk about a buzzkill." She pushed her
glass across the table and gave him the evil eye
until he poured her some more.

He set the bottle down again and decided that
he might as well be honest with her. "Okay, the
way I see it, Gracie, romantic love? It's a crock."

She whipped out a hand and slapped him lightly
on the arm for the second time that evening. "Take
that back."

"Can't. Sorry. What you call love is just an ex-
cuse to misbehave."

"Not true. So wrong."

"Take my parents."

"Dante. Slow down. You're telling me that romantic love's a crock and your parents are your example of why that's so?"

"Exactly."

"But your parents have been married forever and they're *happy*. Aren't they?"

"Blissfully so," he replied in disgust.

"Dante. You're making no sense. I mean, if they're happy, well, isn't that the point?"

"The point is, my mom was seventeen and pregnant with me when she married dad."

"So what? They're happy. They've been married for more than thirty years. Give it a rest."

"They're crazy."

"No."

"Yeah. Crazy in love after all these years. And they always have been. Do you know how many times I walked in on my folks having sex when I was a kid? It was traumatic. No surface was sacred. Apparently, it's still that way." Which was proven out by the fact that a year ago, at the age of forty-eight, his mom had given birth to his littlest brother, Mac. "And look at my sister. Loved your brother since she was barely in her teens. Chased him shamelessly until she finally caught him. Married him. Got wrongly divorced by him. Seven years later, she gets hit in the head and comes running back for more."

Gracie put both her hands out to the side, palms up. "And they're making it work now. They're very happy together, Connor and Aly."

"Romantic love is just another name for insanity." Dante finished off what was left in his glass. "I love my girls. That's a love that matters, a love with dignity and purpose."

She bent down and kissed the top of Owen's hairy head, which was still in her lap. The dog had his eyes closed and a blissed-out expression on his face. "You just haven't met the right woman yet. It will happen."

"No, it won't. The truth is, I'm bad at relationships and I'm just fine with that."

She stuck out that plump lower lip of hers. "That is too sad."

"No, it's not."

"Yes, it is. And I'm sorry it didn't work out with Marjorie. Don't feel bad, Dante."

"Did I say I *feel* bad? I didn't say that. I said I *am* bad at relationships."

"Everyone fails at love."

"Not my parents."

"Okay, *except* for your parents—and my parents, now that I think about it. They were totally in love till the end. And Daniel and Keely. And your brothers, Pascal and Tony, they're happily married, too, right? And let's not forget my sister Aislinn and—"

"Stop." He set his empty glass down harder than necessary. "All these happy couples. I can't take it anymore."

"My point is, you just have to be patient. It will happen. I've been in five failed relationships—if you count Joseph and Randy in high school. And after Paolo, well, I've been going through a bit of a dry spell if you know what I mean, avoiding sex and relationships and all that—but that doesn't mean I'm giving up, you know? I'm just having a break, that's all. I could have a wild fling any day now. And one of these days, I'll find the kind of love your mom and dad have. *I'm* not discouraged."

"Meaning *I* am? I've already said twice that I'm not."

"But you are." She gave Owen another scratch behind the ear. The dog nuzzled her hand and then flopped back down at her feet, rolling to his back in a shameless invitation to another toe massage. Gracie obliged.

Dante watched her pretty, turquoise-painted toes rubbing Owen's belly and laid it out for her *again*. "You're not getting it, Gracie. I'm fine with things just as they are. More than fine."

"But…you never have sex with other people anymore?"

"I didn't say that."

"Ohhh," she said slowly, eyes going wide. "Just flings and hookups, then, is what you're saying?"

"What I'm saying is I like my life. I've got a job that matters, one that interests me, with good potential for advancement." He gestured widely at the trees, the deck, the cliff and the ocean below. "I've got a great house in a beautiful spot, a good dog and most important, two smart, beautiful daughters."

The sun had sunk below the water. It was almost dark. The light by the slider, set on a timer, came on.

Gracie put her hands to her throat and made choking noises.

"Whatever that's supposed to mean," he said flatly, "I don't get it. You need to use words."

"Fine. A life without the prospect of someone special to love just makes me want to strangle myself."

"How many different ways can I say that I'm perfectly happy with how things are?"

"No. Uh-uh. I refuse to believe that you have no interest in finding love again. Dante, you're a great guy. And hot." She peered at him more closely, that pillowy, pink mouth softly parted. "Seriously. You're really hot…" She stood.

Before he could figure out what she was up to, she'd stepped over Owen and plopped down in his lap. With a happy giggle, she wrapped her arms around his neck and stuck her tongue in his ear.

He knew what to do—take her gently but firmly by the arms and hold her away enough that he could look in those big blue eyes and say in a soothing tone, *Gracie. No. Bad idea.*

But there was a problem.

Her tongue in his ear? It felt really good. Almost as good as her pretty, curvy body pressing against him. She smelled fresh and clean and sweet, too. And he liked the way she felt. He liked it a lot. The evidence of how much he liked it was growing beneath his fly. She knew it, too. He could tell by the way she gasped and whispered his name.

Tell her this can't happen, he said to himself.

And he opened his mouth to do that.

But then, her tongue left his ear and her soft lips were right there, meeting his. He sank into that kiss like a drowning man, going down and down, looking up at the sky through the water, realizing that drowning was a good thing—as long as it was Gracie he was drowning in.

Because Gracie, well, she tasted of tequila and

summer and the promise of something so perfect and right.

Of course, it didn't exist, that promise.

He knew that—or rather, the fulfilment of that promise, *that* didn't exist. The promise itself? That was the problem. The promise was so tempting. The promise made the world seem like a much more beautiful place.

And right now, on his back deck, as night came on, just the taste of her mouth and the soft weight of her pretty body and the scent of her skin, it was all magic to him. She practiced the best kind of sorcery, equal parts innocence and heat.

She pulled back a little, but only to slide that mouth of hers along the ridge of his jaw. She gave his chin a little bite.

And then her lips met his again. He went down a second time, plunging below the surface of all his own objections.

Dragging her tightly to him, he speared his tongue into her beautiful mouth. He was drunk, but not *that* drunk. He knew that he shouldn't, that they were friends and this was how friendships ended, that he was violating the very rule he'd once beaten the crap out of Connor for breaking. Because Gracie was Connor's little sister and a guy didn't make moves on his best friend's little sister.

No. Uh-uh. He shouldn't, couldn't, wouldn't…

But she tasted so good, like excellent tequila and the best bad decisions. All the shouldn'ts in the world could not hold out against the flavor of her, the feel of her, so soft and wild, in his arms.

She pulled back violently and blinked at him. "We're both kind of drunk. Maybe this shouldn't be happening. I'm kind of taking advantage of you in a weakened state, aren't I?"

"What the…? Of course not."

"I'm not?"

Wait. He should probably just agree with her, shouldn't he? Put an end to this incredible craziness.

She kissed him again. His brain got all scrambled in the best possible way.

This time, when she put her hands on his shoulders and pulled her mouth from his, she said, "Then again, since we're both hosed, nobody's taking advantage of anybody. It's mutually consensual. Wouldn't you say?" His head started nodding of its own volition. And she gave him her beautiful, glowing smile. "That settles it. We should go inside where the condoms are. You do have condoms, right?"

It was yet another opportunity to tell her they weren't doing this—or even to lie and say he had no condoms. Whatever it took to discourage this completely unacceptable behavior.

This was so wrong. He couldn't have sex with Gracie for any number of reasons, none of which were all that clear to him right at this moment.

And her mouth...

Her mouth was so tempting, all swollen from kissing him. Her skin was flushed a hot, dewy pink and her eyes were the deepest, purest blue.

He scooped her hard against his chest and got up.

"Whoa!" she cried happily, tightening her arms around his neck, kicking her feet a little like she just couldn't contain her glee.

He carried her to the slider. She reached out an arm and pushed it open. Owen went through ahead of them.

Inside, the lights were still on from earlier. Dante turned toward the door again to shut it. Gracie did it for him. Without a word, she pushed it shut and latched it.

His better judgment tried to surface, to put a stop to this insanity. He opened his mouth to gently put the brakes on.

And she kissed him. Her scent was all around him and her skin was so soft, her naughty little tongue all wet and delicious.

His objections flew away. There was nothing in his head now but lust and longing. She felt too perfect in his arms and she tasted like heaven and the scent of her was driving him out of his mind.

Hoisting her higher, he made for the hallway that led to the bedrooms.

Chapter Two

Grace woke to morning light.

She opened her eyes and saw Dante, sound asleep on the other pillow, his eyelashes so thick and black against his tanned cheeks. He looked really peaceful.

And that made her smile.

How much tequila had they drunk? A lot. She deserved to have a hangover—a headache, at least.

But she didn't.

Gently, so as not to wake him, she rolled to her back and shut her eyes. Her smile got wider.

Seriously, what a night.

And with Dante. Who knew? Yeah, she'd always considered him hot. But way too controlled. He wasn't a happy man, really—a good man, but not happy. She'd always assumed he was the kind of guy who would have trouble getting loose in bed.

Wrong.

She sighed in pure bliss as X-rated scenes from the night before played out on the dark screen of her eyelids.

After the first go-round, which had been nothing short of spectacular, they'd raided his freezer and gobbled Tillamook Mudslide straight from the carton, each with a spoon, passing the chunky chocolate deliciousness back and forth. He'd then ordered her to drink more water to prevent a hangover later. She'd laughed and called him a control freak, but she did drink the water.

Gracie frowned. About then, he'd started acting kind of distant, hadn't he? She'd had a really bad feeling he was going to start backing off, start saying that maybe it hadn't been such a smart idea for them to fall into bed together.

But she'd known how to shut him up about that.

She'd kissed him. Worked like a charm. He scooped her right up and carried her back down the hall to his bed, where the good times rolled some more.

Sometime after midnight, they'd fallen asleep. She'd closed her eyes for a minute—and slept straight through until morning.

What a night.

She could not wait to do it all again.

Carefully, so as not to wake him, she eased her legs over the side of the bed and slid out from under the covers. Her clothes were right there on the bedside chair. She put them on swiftly and tiptoed to the door.

Sweet Owen was waiting on the other side. Pulling the bedroom door silently shut behind her, she asked in a whisper, "Need to go out, boy?"

He let out a low whine and turned to lead the way.

Outside, she found her pink Chuck Taylors right there on the deck by her chair, where she'd left them. Her purse was there, too, still hanging on the back of her chair. She put on the Chucks, hooked the purse over her shoulder and walked Owen into the trees to do his business. As she trailed along behind him, she got out her phone to check messages.

There were two texts from Daniel asking if she was all right.

Oops. They had an agreement that if she wasn't coming home, she would let him know she was okay—and he would refrain from asking questions about what she'd been doing and with whom.

She answered, Sorry. A little too much tequila at Dante Santangelo's place. Stayed here to be safe. (And to have the best sex ever in the history of sex. But her big brother didn't need that kind of TMI.) I'm fine. Home in a while.

He responded right away. Okay, then. Thanks for letting me know.

Was he pissed at her? Probably. Daniel hated it when she didn't keep her agreements. But she was going to call this a win. She'd messed up and he'd been civil about it when she apologized.

It could've been so much worse.

On the way back inside, she grabbed the remains of their dinner, the glasses and the nearly empty bottle from last night.

In the kitchen, Owen went straight to his food bowl. He sniffed at it and then looked up at her with those sad doggy eyes. She took the hint and found him a can of dog stew in the pantry closet. After dishing the food into his bowl, she freshened up his water.

"Good, huh?" She stood over him as he wolfed down his meal. "And now I need coffee."

Dante had one of those pod machines. She loaded up some Peet's French Roast.

Five minutes later, she was standing at the counter savoring that first cup when Dante, in jeans and a fresh T-shirt, emerged from the back of the house.

She watched him come toward her, her heart lifting just at the sight of him.

God, he was gorgeous. All that thick, wavy almost-black hair, those smoldering eyes. The eight-pack, the V-lines, the ebony treasure trail leading to fun and fulfilment—and no, she couldn't see all that amazingness right now. But she *had* seen it and thoroughly enjoyed it last night. It was all burned into her brain in the best sort of way.

And then she met his dark eyes. Instantly, she *knew*. It was so painfully clear to her before he even opened his mouth.

Mr. Control was back with a vengeance.

"Hey," he said.

"Hey."

He knelt to give his dog a good-morning scratch down his back and a pat on the head. "You found the coffee all right?"

As if that even required an answer. She raised her mug to him as he rose. Sliding to the side a little, she made room for him at the coffee maker.

The silence had weight as he loaded the machine and put his cup under the spout. He pushed the button and turned around to lean against the counter as it brewed.

For a good thirty seconds, they stood there, side by side, the coffee maker gurgling and hissing behind him. She drank her coffee and waited. It seemed only fair to give him a chance to *not* disappoint her.

"Gracie, I…" The sentence wandered off unfinished.

Okay, yeah. Message received. He regretted last night and was about to tell her all about how it could never happen again.

Well, okay then. He would say what he had to say. As for Gracie, she refused to help him in any way, shape or form. She enjoyed her coffee and waited for the rest.

"Gracie, will you look at me?"

Stifling a sigh, she turned her head to face him. Those melty brown eyes were full of self-recrimination and regret.

"I'm sorry," he said. "I never should have touched you. I'm too old for you and I'm not any kind of relationship material, anyway. I don't know what got into me, but I swear to you it's never going to happen again."

Hmm. How to respond?

Too bad there wasn't a large blunt object nearby. The guy deserved a hard bop on head. What was *wrong* with him? No wonder it hadn't worked out with Marjorie. The man didn't have a clue.

But never mind. Gracie held it together as he apologized some more. She watched that beautiful mouth move and pondered the mystery of how such a great guy could have his head so far up his own ass.

Maybe if she yanked him close and kissed him, he'd get over himself and admit that last night had been amazing, the two of them had off-the-charts chemistry and he didn't want to walk away from all that goodness, after all.

Yeah, kissing him might shut him up and get him back on track for more hot, sexy times. It had worked more than once already.

But come on. She couldn't go jumping on him and smashing her mouth on his every time he started beating himself up for having a good time with her.

No. A girl had to have a little pride.

He thought last night was a mistake?

Fair enough. She'd actually let herself believe for a minute or two there that they had something good going on, that her long dry spell man-wise might be over.

But never mind about that. Let him have it his way. She would agree with him.

And then she would show him exactly what he was missing. And *then*, when he couldn't take it anymore and begged her for another chance, she would say that they *couldn't*, that he was too *old* for her and it wouldn't be *right*.

Not that she was vindictive or anything...

"You're right, Dante," she said with exaggerated sincerity. "It was a big mistake. One that can never happen again—and about the cabin? I'll take it. You are a lifesaver. Thank you so much."

For a fraction of a second, he looked kind of stunned. But then he gave a solemn nod. "Well, all right then."

"Is there furniture out there already or will I need to bring my own?" She could use her bedroom suite from Daniel's. Plus, Daniel and Keely had a lot of random pieces stored in the attic and basement of the Bravo house. Getting the cabin furnished wouldn't be a problem.

"There's a bed, a table, a chest of drawers, some chairs and some kitchen stuff." He moved down the counter, took something from a drawer and came back to her. "Here you go." He handed her a key, which she stuck in a pocket of her cutoffs. "Anything that's in there you don't need, no problem. I've got space to store it."

"That'll work. I'm off from the Sea Breeze again today, so I was thinking I would just go ahead and move in."

He frowned. She was sure he would start backpedaling, saying maybe they ought to rethink this, that now they'd shared a night of fabulous sex, it wasn't such a good idea for her to live on his property.

But in the end, he said only, "All right. I've got today and tomorrow off. I'll help."

"Thanks, but I can handle it." She would need to scare up a truck and get one of her brothers to take on the heavy lifting. If none of them were available, she had friends. Someone would come to her rescue.

Dante scowled. "I said I would help. We can use my pickup."

She gave a him big smile. Really, he was a terrific man—well, aside from that stick up his butt. "I hate to keep taking *advantage* of you."

"You're not. Come on, let me help."

"Then thank you. Again."

He still looked way too serious. "Gracie, is this going to wreck our friendship?"

She had such a deep longing to make him squirm. It took serious effort to not put on an innocent voice and probe a little, ask him what, exactly, he meant by *this*?

But no. If she did that, he might just tell her. "No, it's not going to wreck anything. Not for me, anyway." She met his eyes straight on. Was he going to insist they talk about it? Really, the last thing she needed right now was Dante getting down in the weeds with all the reasons last night couldn't, shouldn't, wouldn't be happening again. "Your coffee's ready."

"Right." He gave a slow nod and took his full mug from under the spout. For a moment, they just stood there, sipping and staring at anything but each other.

Finally, he offered, "How 'bout some breakfast?"

"I would love some."

After they ate, Dante showed Gracie the cabin.

She walked in the door, took a slow look around and said, "I love it," which made him feel pretty damn terrific in spite of his doubts about having her living so close after last night. "There's room for a sitting area *and* my bed, not to mention it has an actual kitchen."

The kitchen consisted of a small range and a compact fridge with a counter and cabinets between them, a sink in the middle. "It's pretty basic," he said.

"Don't you disrespect my new kitchen," she commanded, looking way too adorable in those damn sexy Daisy Dukes and that T-shirt that exposed her flat stomach and clung to those fine breasts he wouldn't be fondling again. "Everything's so clean, too."

"I got a Groupon for cleaning services a couple of weeks ago. I had them go through the house and then went ahead and paid extra for them to clean this place, too—never hurts to get rid of the cobwebs now and then."

"There's even a window above the sink." She leaned over the sink to peer outside, causing her right butt cheek to peek out from under the tattered hem of those cutoffs that really ought to be illegal. He gritted his teeth and ordered himself to forget about last night and simply appreciate the spectacular view of her shapely behind. "Perfect," she said with a happy little sigh.

Next, she went through the cabinets and got all enthusiastic about pots and pans, dishes, mismatched glassware and the drawer of utensils and flatware. He watched her bending to look in the lower cupboards and stretching to peer in the high ones. Her butt cheek reappeared more than once and that damn T-shirt kept drawing tight across those breasts he needed to stop staring at.

"I'll keep the sofa," she said, "and the drop-leaf kitchen table and chairs." She wanted to bring her own bedroom furniture. "You said you have somewhere you can put this bed and bureau?"

"No problem. There's a shed behind the garage. Plenty of room in there."

She babbled on, all sunny enthusiasm, about planting rhododendrons by the front door and a rag rug she thought might be stored in the attic at the Bravo house. "That rug would so tie the room together."

He agreed to all of it. Whatever she wanted. Because she was a friend and a guy helped his friends. Even if, after last night, he was never going to be able to look at her and not see her naked inside his head.

She looked incredible without any clothes on, all that pale, firm skin. Her whole body flushed the prettiest shade of pink when she was turned on.

But he wasn't going to think of that. From this moment on, he was wiping thoughts of Gracie Bravo naked right out of his brain.

He plugged in the fridge. Together, they moved

the chest of drawers and the bed to the shed. Then
he followed her in his pickup to the Bravo house
up on Rhinehart Hill. Daniel wasn't there. Keely
was, though, along with the kids and Ingrid Oster-
gard, who was Keely's mother and also the owner
of the Sea Breeze bar where Gracie worked.

Keely took Gracie's arm. "We need to talk."

"You're right," Gracie agreed.

The two women vanished into Gracie's room
off the kitchen, leaving Dante with Ingrid, the
twins, Frannie and Jake, and the toddler, Marie.
The twins were busy making what looked like
a village of Duplo blocks over by the breakfast nook, the family basset hound stretched out
nearby. Marie toddled Dante's way and kind of
landed against his leg. She was a cute little thing,
with wispy strawberry curls.

She beamed up at him, causing a tightness in
his chest as he thought of his daughters. It seemed
just yesterday they'd been Marie's age. "Up." So he
swung her up in his arms and she patted his face
and babbled out nonsense syllables. "You don't
say?" he asked. She babbled some more and he
nodded. "No kidding…"

Ingrid, who had green hair this week and wore
a purple tank top, sat over at the breakfast nook
table. She'd been the lead singer and guitarist for

a one-hit wonder rock band back in the eighties. Now she lived with her widowed sister, Gretchen Snow. "Gracie tell you I'm losing her come September?"

"She did. She seems excited to start teaching." He caught Marie's fat little hand before she could poke him in the eye.

"I hate to see her go. But you can't keep the good ones forever, you know?"

Unfortunately, he'd had Gracie for only one night—way short of forever. And maybe "had" was the wrong word. Too objectifying. Or something.

"Dante?" Ingrid seemed to be hiding a grin. "You with me?"

"Uh. Yeah—and you're right. Good things never last forever." *Some of them last only one damn night.*

"Gwamma Ingwid," said Frannie, with a Duplo in each hand. "Come help."

Ingrid, who was slim and fit and maybe in her fifties, got up and joined the twins on the floor.

Gracie emerged from the short hall next to the pantry, Keely right behind her. "I'll head up to Warrenton, tell him in person," Gracie said. Dante knew she meant Daniel. Her eldest brother ran Valentine Logging. The family company had its offices on the Columbia at the Warrenton docks. "Just as soon as we get all my things into the cabin at Dante's."

"That'll work," agreed Keely.

Gracie shifted her glance to Dante. He felt the force of her gaze all through him. Did he have it bad for her? He decided it was better not to think about that.

She asked, "Ready to haul some heavy furniture out to your truck?"

"I'm ready." He put Marie down and she toddled over to join the Duplo builders on the floor. "Let's get after it."

She led him back to her room and they got to work taking the bed apart.

A few hours later, they had her bedroom furniture and all of Gracie's clothes and random other stuff loaded into the two vehicles. They caravanned back to his place and transferred everything into the cabin. Dante had had a graveled side driveway added a few years ago. It branched off to the cabin from the main driveway, so they were able to drive right up to the cabin door.

By a little after three, they had everything out of the vehicles and stacked up in the cabin, ready to be put away. He helped her reassemble the bed.

Once that was done, she fell back across the mattress with a groan that made him start think-

ing about last night again—not that he'd ever really stopped. "Thank you so much, Dante. You're
a lifesaver on so many levels. Now, I'm going to
see if I can find a towel and a bar of soap in one of
those boxes somewhere. I'll take a quick shower
and then go tell my big brother that a miracle has
happened and I've found somewhere other than
the room off his kitchen to live."

He realized he was starving. They hadn't eaten
since the eggs and sausage they'd had at breakfast.
"Come on over to the house first. I've got plenty
of stuff for sandwiches. You should eat."

She remained sprawled across the bed, looking way too inviting, with her arms thrown out
wide, her pink Chucks dangling an inch from the
floor. "Can't."

Owen, who had followed them around as they
brought in her things, trotted over to her, dropped
to his haunches and whined at her hopefully.

She sat up and gave him a pat on the head. With
her free hand, she pulled the elastic free of her high
ponytail. The silvery mass spilled over shoulders
and down her back. He wanted to grab her arm,
yank her up off the bed, wrap her hair around his
fist and pull her head back so he could bite her
smooth, pale neck.

"I need to get going," she said. "I want to catch Daniel before he heads for home."

"It's been hours since breakfast." He should shut up. He sounded like some fussy old mother hen. But then he just kept on talking. "You've got to be hungry and you really should eat."

She laughed. The happy sound kind of reached down inside him, making him yearn for something he was never going to have. Between completely unacceptable bouts of pure lust for her, he kept thinking that maybe they should talk about what had happened last night, kind of clear the air a little, get their friendship back on track. But then, what were they going to say?

No. It was probably better to just leave it alone.

"I'll grab a burger on the way," she said. "Promise. Don't worry about me. I'm fine."

If she wanted to starve herself, how was he going to stop her? He let it go.

She thanked him again. He clicked his tongue at Owen and the dog followed him back to the main house.

At the Warrenton docks, Gracie went straight to the barnlike building where Valentine Logging had its offices. Daniel was still there. The office manager told her to go on in.

A big man, broad shouldered and square jawed, with hair a little darker than her own, Daniel sat at his desk punching keys on his laptop. He glanced up at her when she entered. "Scotch?"

"No, thanks." Daniel always brought out the good Scotch during important discussions, to mark life transitions and for big occasions. Apparently, he already knew why she was here. "Keely told you, huh?"

He rose, went to the liquor cart in the corner and poured himself a small one. "She said you'd be dropping by. I asked what was going on. She said you would explain everything."

"You don't know what I'm here for and you offered the good Scotch anyway?"

He saluted her with his glass. "Just in case I'm going to need it."

She laughed. "Yeah. I get that. You never know what kind of crap I might pull next."

He had on his wary face. "I didn't say that."

"But maybe you thought it?" She held up her thumb and forefinger with a sliver of space between them. "Just a little…"

He went to the sofa and chairs across from his desk and gestured for her to join him as he sat. She took one of the chairs and Daniel said, "So what's going on?"

"Dante Santangelo offered me this little cabin he has on his property. I took it. Moved all my stuff in there today."

He asked, very carefully, "So, you and Dante…?"

She almost gave him a dirty look, but somehow managed to stop herself in time. "We're friends." *Yeah, okay. With benefits—for last night only and never again.* But all that was TMI as far as her big brother was concerned. "We got to know each other at the bar. He likes to stop in there for a beer a couple of times a week."

Daniel now looked thoughtful, like maybe he was pondering the mysteries of the universe. "Dante's a good man."

She realized then that this conversation was actually going well. Her overbearing eldest brother was treating her like an adult. And that was the second time he'd seemed to imply that maybe she and Dante had a thing. And they kind of did. A very short thing that Daniel never needed to know about. "Like I said, Dante's a friend."

Daniel studied her for several seconds, long enough that she almost started to worry about what he might say next. But then he only reminded her gently, "Your room is there for you. Come home to stay anytime you need to."

Her throat clutched. Just a little. "I'm going to

try really hard not to. You should use my room for a guest room. It's downstairs, private, with its own bath. I already took all my furniture and stuff, so you don't even need to clear it out."

"It's not going to be the same without you there." His voice was kind of gruff. Like he might be just a little choked up, too.

Strange. It seemed like she and Daniel had been at odds since she turned ten or so. But right now, all she felt was affection for him—and gratitude that he'd kept them all together, kept them a family, when their parents died.

"I'm sorry that we haven't always gotten along. I think my moving out on my own will be good, you know?"

"Yeah."

It was the right time, she realized, to tell him what she really thought of him. "You are amazing and strong and we all count on you far too much. I love you a lot, Daniel."

He gave her a slow nod. "And I love you. I'm proud of you, too, Gracie. You do things your own way and I'm slowly learning to accept that you're all grown up, not my little baby sister anymore."

When she got up to leave, he held out his arms. She stepped into them and they shared a hug.

"You need help with the move?" he asked.

"Thanks, but no. It's handled."

"Whatever I can do, you just let me know."

"That works both ways." She smiled up at him, feeling really good about everything right at that moment.

Grace stopped for a burger and then to get groceries before heading back to the cabin. It was a little after seven and she'd almost finished putting the food away when someone tapped on the door.

She figured it would be Dante.

And it was.

Sweet Lord, he looked good. All dark and broody. He must have showered. His tanned cheeks were clean-shaven, he smelled of some yummy aftershave and he'd changed to black jeans and a faded plaid shirt with the sleeves rolled up to reveal those sculpted forearms of his.

"Just the man I wanted to see," she said. "I have something for you."

His dark eyebrows drew together in a worried frown. "What?"

"So suspicious," she chided, and ushered him in. Owen was right behind him. "Here you go." She had a check already made out to him, but when she took it from her pocket, he put up both hands like she'd pulled a gun on him.

"Gracie. Come on. I said that's not necessary."

"It's the five hundred I was going to pay Sonja."

"Keep it."

"No."

"Gracie…"

"Listen. I know it's hardly what a homey little cabin in the woods with a nearby trail leading down to a gorgeous stretch of beach would bring you if you actually rented it out, but at least it'll cover utilities."

"I said no. Forget it."

"Five hundred a month," she repeated, her chin high. "If you don't take it, that's a deal breaker. You'll be forcing me to load all this stuff into my Toyota and move back to Daniel's. And you know that will be bad for the Bravo family dynamic. I love my big brother and he loves me, but it's definitely time for me *not* to be living in his house." Dante had lowered his hands by then. She grabbed one and slapped the check in it.

He looked down at the scrap of paper and then back up at her. Owen, who'd dropped to his haunches at their feet, whined up at them.

"It's okay, boy," she said to the dog. "Your human is stubborn, but we're working it out."

Annoyance flashed in Dante's eyes and his gorgeous high cheekbones suddenly looked like they might poke right through his skin. "You're not going to give the hell up on this are you?"

"Nope. And you need to cash that in the next few days. Unless you'd really rather I didn't stay here. If you don't cash it, I'll know you want me gone and I'll make that happen."

"See how you did that? You turned it all around on me. If I don't take your money, I want you gone?"

"So, then. You *don't* want me gone?"

"Of course not." He really seemed to mean it.

And she felt considerable relief. She had kind of worried that after last night, he would prefer that she lived elsewhere. "Good, then," she answered softly. "Five hundred a month."

He threw up both hands again. "Have it your way."

"Thank you. It's a steal and we both know it. So much better than a room in someone's house." She went back to the kitchen counter to finish emptying the last grocery bag.

He was silent. A quick glance over her shoulder confirmed that he was just standing there in the middle of the room, surrounded by plastic bags and a few boxes and more than one suitcase full of her stuff.

"What can I do to help?" he asked.

She stuck a giant box of Cinnamon Toast Crunch in the cupboard and turned to him. "You helped me all day. Go home. Take a break. Head on over to the Sea Breeze for a beer."

He didn't budge, just stood there frowning at the piles of stuff she'd yet to put away. "You eat something?"

"Yes, *Mother*, I did."

"You must be exhausted."

She wasn't, not really. She'd always had a lot of energy. And she was excited to have her own space at last. It was beautiful here. Maybe, before bed, she would take the trail down to the beach, enjoy a stroll along the shore. "I think I'm getting my second wind. And hey, the bed's made." It had stacks of towels and two suitcases on it, though. "When I get tired, I can just shove everything off it and climb in."

Now he was staring down at the rag rug, which they'd left rolled up near the sofa when they brought it in from his truck. "Let's roll the rug out, why don't we?"

She braced her hands on her hips. "You just can't stop helping, can you?"

He flashed her a mouthful of straight white teeth and she swooned a little inside. "Please. You know you need a hand moving the furniture out of the way."

She really could use some help with the rug. "Well, since you asked so nicely…"

They set to work, shoving the bed, the nightstand, the coffee table and all her stuff against the walls, rolling the rug out, positioning it just so, and then putting the furniture in place on top of it.

"It looks so good," she said, standing back by the window to admire the effect. "My great-great-grandmother Cora Valentine made this rug as part of her trousseau." The braided rug was a treasure, with a rainbow of colors woven into it. "So cozy and homey."

Dante had already moved on to the next job. The two suitcases were still on the bed. He grabbed one and pulled it to the edge of the mattress. "We should clear off the bed, figure out where you want all this stuff to go."

She knew what was in that suitcase and almost stopped him. But then she remembered the little promise she'd made to herself.

Really, she shouldn't.

He'd gone way above and beyond to help her out when she needed a hand, not only providing a place for her, but pitching right in to help her make it habitable. The guy was a true friend.

Even if he had given her a speeding ticket.

It wasn't right for her to hold a grudge just because he said he wouldn't have sex with her again.

But, well, some grudges were too much fun to give up.

And besides, Dante Santangelo was wound way too tight. He needed to loosen the heck up.

Grace was only too happy to help him with that. She crossed the space between them and stood at his side.

He unzipped the suitcase and tossed the lid back, revealing stacks of pretty bras, sexy panties and a froth of different nighties she hardly ever wore. For a moment, he stared down at all those goodies—not embarrassed, exactly.

More like not sure where to take it from there.

"I confess," she said wryly. "I've got this thing for lingerie. I've controlled my fancy-panty addiction the past year or so in my ongoing effort to get the budget under control, but I still have more undies than will fit in my drawers—if you know what I mean." She snatched up a fuchsia-pink satin thong and another pair of panties that was mostly lace. "What do you think—a thong?" She dangled the bit of satin by her index finger. "Or cheekies?" She waved the black lace.

He gave her a look of great patience, with just

maybe a touch of sexy smolder there in his eyes. "All your drawers are full, you said?"

"Yup." She popped the *p* and pressed both pairs of panties to her breasts. "What shall I *do*?"

Dante was all business. "I say we bring back that bureau from the shed." He pointed to a bare corner next to the window on the other side of the bed. "It should fit there."

She gave him a blinding smile. "Brilliant."

And really now, exactly how far should she take this? He didn't seem to have noticed yet, but tucked in with all that lace and silk and satin was a personal pleasure toy—or five. Because a girl who's steering clear of romantic complications for a while definitely needs a little stimulation now and then.

She was just about to grab her favorite magic wand and wave it at him with gleeful enthusiasm when he said, "Let's go get it, then." And turned for the door.

They brought the bureau back.

Again, she tried to tell him he'd done enough.

But he refused to stop there. He helped her empty the big black plastic bags, the other suitcase and the boxes. Somehow, they found a place for everything. As for her lingerie and personal pleasure devices, he steered clear of them, so she put them away herself without brandishing a single one.

He didn't go back to the main house until after nine.

She stood at the door as he left. "I can't believe I'm pretty much moved in already. Thank you. Again."

"Anytime. Come on, Owen." His dog at his heels, Dante headed off through the trees.

She watched him stride along the footpath until he reached the cleared area that surrounded his house. No, she hadn't given up on her plan to drive him mad with unsatisfied lust.

But that was going to take time. He was a tough nut to crack. Luckily, she lived here now and would have all sorts of opportunities to work on bringing him to his knees, sexually speaking.

Operation Make Dante Beg for It was going to be a whole lot of fun.

Chapter Three

Dante stood at the slider that led out to the deck. Staring out past the twisted trees that framed the path down to the beach, he watched the last orange fingers of sunset fade into the growing dark.

He'd seen those sex toys of hers.

How could he miss them? One was two-pronged and purple and one was as aggressively pink as that thong she'd dangled at him from her finger. One even looked like a microphone.

At least she'd put them away in the bureau without making a show of them. Her sudden attack of discretion had surprised him. After all, she'd asked him about his preference in panties, hadn't she?

He'd figured she wouldn't pass up the chance to taunt him with her, er, sensual devices.

But even without all the sexy underthings and the battery-powered pleasure enhancers, the woman would still be driving him insane. He wanted to touch her, pull her close, kiss those beautiful, bubblegum-pink lips of hers. He wanted to spend a couple of hours sitting out on the deck in the light of the moon with her. He wanted to whisper with her about nothing in particular, to listen to her laugh and bask in her bright, gorgeous smiles.

It all sounded so damn romantic.

And it wasn't going to happen.

He'd really messed up. He'd had too much tequila and then given in to the urge to have sex with someone he considered a friend, someone he cared about who he didn't want to lose. Now he wanted his friend back, at the same time as he was never going to forget the way she looked naked.

And that moment with the panties? She *had* been tormenting him on purpose. He knew that she had.

She was young and free-spirited. So different from him on so many levels. That she had no shame about provoking him with her sexy underwear was just more proof of all the ways the two of them were not any kind of a match—not that he was even looking for a match in the first place.

He'd meant what he told her last night. His life worked just fine as it was and trying for something meaningful with a woman was more likely to screw everything up than to make things better.

They were friends, damn it. He shouldn't have slept with her, though he couldn't quite bring himself to regret that he had. It had been nothing short of perfect, spending the night with Gracie. The sex was mind-blowing and yet, she was still Gracie, with her smart mouth and her bubbly laugh. Gracie, who, as it turned out, felt just right in his arms.

But that was last night and last night was over.

All he wanted now was to still be her friend and put last night behind them.

And he would. Over time.

Because, come on. It had been less than twenty-four hours since he'd had her in his bed. The powerful desire to do it again was bound to fade as the days went by. He'd gotten her settled in at the cabin. Now all he had to do was steer clear of her for a while, give his mind and his body some distance. Let that distance solve the problem for him.

It was all going to work out just fine.

Since he'd made detective, Dante mostly worked day shifts, and then was on call at night for major crimes, of which there were few in Valentine Bay.

However, when he didn't have his daughters with him, he tried to be flexible, help the other guys out so they would have his back scheduling-wise when Nat and Nic were home.

As a result, he'd taken C Watch for the next five days, 10:00 p.m. to 6:30 in the morning. In Valentine Bay, night watch was about fighting boredom more than anything else. Now and then you got a rough domestic to sort out or a burglary to solve or drunks acting up, but it was hardly like some big-city departments where you took your life in your hands every night on the street.

Working all night had a side benefit this time around. For five days straight, he got home at 9:00 a.m., after an hour at the gym and then breakfast. He would sleep until late afternoon. That meant he'd have little opportunity to see Gracie. She worked either early afternoon to ten at night, or six to closing. They were on completely different schedules. All he had to do was *not* stop in at the Sea Breeze and he would never see her.

Out of sight, out of mind. Right?

Except he couldn't stop thinking about her.

Plus, well, she was right there in front of him most afternoons, planting rhododendrons outside the cabin in a tiny little top that showed off her flat stomach and those battered jean shorts that ought to be illegal. Or heading down to the beach in a swimsuit made of what looked like three tiny handkerchiefs and a few pieces of string.

Apparently, she had the closing shift at the bar that week, leaving all afternoon and most of the evening for him to spot her outside. And really, he knew way more than he should about her schedule, didn't he? Plus, he found himself looking out the damn windows constantly now. Never in his life had he felt like a creeper.

Until now.

Also, there was Owen. The damn dog was in love with her and had grown nothing short of crafty about slipping out any door Dante opened and heading for the cabin. If she was home, Gracie would bring him back, which was nice of her. He would order the dog inside, thank her and shut the door on her, knowing that he was being borderline rude to her.

But it was hard enough on his equilibrium staring at her out a window when he shouldn't be, trying not to think of what she looked like naked. Up close, it was even harder—*hard* being the operative word.

Saturday afternoon, she called him to tell him she had a leaky pipe under the bathroom sink. "I stuck a pot under it, but it's not looking good. I need either a bigger pot, to stop using the sink or to hire a plumber," she said. "I'm happy to handle it. Word on the street is that Santangelo Plumbing is the best around. I'll just call them if that's okay?"

"Word on the street is right for once." His dad had inherited the plumbing business from his father before him. "But I'll take care of it." He'd worked alongside his father in the summers back in high school and to bring in extra cash when he and Marjorie first got married.

"How 'bout soon?" she asked hopefully.

"How 'bout now?"

"Works for me."

When he got there, she was wearing a short kimono-type robe and just possibly nothing under it. She knelt to pet Owen, and Dante tried not to look down at her sleek bare legs and the way the top of the robe kind of gaped where it wrapped between her breasts.

"I was about to take a shower when I saw the water on the floor." And that had him picturing her naked in the shower—really, there were so many ways he could picture her naked. The possibilities were endless. And he needed to cease and desist on that front.

She rose. "Come on. I'll show you." He tried really hard not to stare at the rounded perfection of her ass beneath the revealing silk of her robe as he followed her into the bathroom, where the door to the small cabinet under the sink was wide open.

He flipped on the water and then knelt to watch the water drip into the pot. The seals had failed in at least two places. Reaching in there, he turned the valves at the back wall that shut off the water to the faucet.

"If I patch the joints, it will probably just start leaking again, so I'm going to replace the whole assembly," he said as he stood. "I'll need to run to the hardware store to get parts."

She stood by the door, barefooted in her short kimono, her arms wrapped around her middle. "Can I go ahead and shower while you're gone? I'll make it quick." Owen, seated at her side, his floppy tongue hanging out, panted and gazed up at her adoringly. Really, how could Dante blame the damn dog for panting over her. She was too tempting by half.

"Dante?" She asked again. "Is it okay if I have a shower?"

He gave himself a mental shake. "Uh, sure. I've turned the water off under the sink, so you can't use that faucet, but the shower's a go."

"You have to work tonight?"

"Ten to six thirty."

She chewed on the corner of her full lower lip. "And there goes the rest of your afternoon and evening. Sorry."

As though he had anything all that important to do. He didn't—and that was another thing having her around made him all too acutely aware of: life was short and he was spending way too much of it just kind of going through the motions.

Okay, yeah. He was set in his ways and not likely to change. But having Gracie around sure made life a lot more interesting.

Was she trying to drive him a little bit crazy with her Daisy Dukes and that short kimono that gaped in the front when she bent down and showed off her spectacular behind every time she turned around? With her teasing smiles and come-and-get-it glances—not to mention her sexy underwear and personal pleasure devices?

Probably.

Right at the moment, though, he kind of hoped she never stopped.

Which made him only too happy to spend his afternoon fixing the drainpipe under the sink for her. He liked doing things for her. On top of the whole burning-lust thing he had going on for her, he also wanted to take her in his arms and reassure her—of what, exactly, he had no idea. What-ever she needed, he wanted to make sure she got it.

At the same time, he'd made it his mission *not* to give in to his consuming need to grab her close and peel off whatever skimpy piece of nothing she happened to be wearing at any given moment.

"Not your fault," he said. "Pipes leak now and then. It's a fact of life."

The trip to the hardware store took almost an hour. When he got back, the cabin smelled like trop-ical flowers, probably from her shower gel. She was dressed in dark-wash jeans and a Sea Breeze T-shirt, all ready for work.

"I need to get going," she said. "It's summer and it's Saturday. We're packed from four or so straight through till closing. Ingrid needs all hands on deck."

And he felt let down, though he'd been avoid-ing her all week. "No problem. I'll lock up when I'm done."

"Thanks—oh, and one other thing." She grabbed an envelope off the counter. It was addressed and had a stamp on it. "My check for that ticket you gave me. Can I just drop it in the slot of that group mailbox near the end of your driveway?"

"That'll work."

"Great." She knelt to give Owen a quick cuddle.

A moment later, she was at the door. Turning back to him, she asked, "You doing all right, Dante?"

"Of course," he said too quickly and then made it worse by adding, "Fine. Why?"

She gave him this sweet little smile, kind of tender and knowing. "When's your next night off?"

"Tuesday."

"Perfect. I'm off Tuesday, too. Let me cook you dinner. Show my appreciation. For the cabin and the, er…"

"Do not make a dirty joke about your plumbing," he warned.

She stifled a giggle and then tried to look innocent. "Never, ever would I do such a thing. So, Tuesday? Dinner?"

He shouldn't encourage her—except there was nothing in the world he would rather do than spend his night off with her. "I would like that."

"Terrific. You're on."

Sunday, Grace went to dinner with the family at the Bravo house. Her brother Connor and his wife, Aly, Dante's only sister, came, too. They brought their month-old daughter, Emelia.

The baby was the center of attention. Everyone wanted to hold her, including Grace. After dinner, she finally got a chance to have that baby in her arms.

"She is gorgeous." Grace held Emelia's tiny hand and kissed her perfect miniature nose.

Aly said, "She's a handful, but in the best way possible—I heard you moved into that little cabin at my brother's place."

"Yeah. I love it. It's gorgeous there and the cabin is nice. I feel right at home."

"He treating you right?"

What, exactly, did Aly mean by that? Grace answered cautiously. "He's a good friend—and he would have let me have the cabin for free. I had to twist his arm to get him to take what I would've paid for a room in someone's house."

"A good friend, huh?"

Grace smoothed the blanket around the baby's adorable, squinty little face and looked up to meet Aly's eyes directly. "Okay, whatever you're getting at, just go ahead and say it."

It was only the three of them—the baby, Grace and Aly—on one end of the big sofa in the family room. Everyone else was still hanging out at the table in the dining room or in the backyard or grouped around the island in Keely's big kitchen.

Aly said quietly, "Connor and I saw you together."

"Me and Dante?" Except for a few hours last Tuesday night, they'd never been "together" anywhere that she could remember. At least not "together" the way Aly seemed to imply. "When?"

"Last summer, at the Sea Breeze. You looked—I don't know. It was just a moment. You were behind the bar and he was getting a pitcher or something. You were both laughing. There was this energy, you know, a certain chemistry between you. It was pretty obvious. I thought so and Connor did, too. He was really pissed off."

"Why?"

Aly shrugged. "Can I just say it's a guy thing and leave it at that?"

"Sure. I suppose…"

"You'll be happy to know I got all up in Connor's face about it and he ended up agreeing that it was your business—yours and Dante's—and he would stay out of it." Now Aly grinned. "I don't know what it is with guys sometimes, but I make it my mission to call them on their stupid crap whenever necessary."

"The women of the world are grateful—me included. But you said this happened last summer? Wow." That seemed forever ago. Absolutely nothing romantic had been going on between Grace and Dante back then. And there was nothing going on between them now, either. Because Dante considered himself too old for her, and because he didn't do relationships. Grace slowly shook her head. "We really are just friends."

Aly laughed. She leaned in close and whispered, "I so do not believe that. If Dante hasn't made a move on you, he's a fool."

"You don't think I'm too young for him?"

"No way. You're just what he needs. A little joy and sunshine in his life for a change. And that's nothing against his ex, either. Marjorie's a good person. It was just…not really happening with the two of them, you know? They'd broken up. It was over. She'd moved back to Portland. But then it turned out she was pregnant with the twins, so they got married at the county clerk's office and tried to make it work."

"I didn't know."

Aly forked her hands back through her thick dark hair. "Dante will be giving me hell when he finds out I told you that."

"I won't say anything to him."

"No worries." Aly waved a hand. "Honesty is the way to go, I believe that. Tell him what I said. Dante and me, we're always getting into it. I can handle my brother. He gives me grief, I give it right back to him. He's a good man and he means well.

But he thinks he knows how things should be and at least half the time, he's wrong."

On Tuesday, Dante got up at three in the afternoon. Outside, the sun was shining and he had a really strong sense of…what?

Promise, maybe.

Anticipation.

He reminded himself not to be an idiot. It was just dinner and nothing was going to happen between him and Gracie tonight—or ever again. He wouldn't let it.

But that didn't mean they couldn't enjoy each other's company now and then, did it?

They were friends and friends spent time together.

He made coffee and wandered around the house in old sweats and a Portland State T-shirt, thinking he probably ought to get dressed and drive over to his mom's house for a quick visit, see how she and his eight-and-a-half-month-old brother, Mac, were doing. But the coffee tasted really good and he was enjoying being lazy on his day off.

He ended up standing at the sink, looking out the kitchen window, staring at the trees and the gravel driveway leading to the cabin. As he watched, Gracie emerged. She wore busted-out jeans and one of those silky cami tops. It was printed with big tropical flowers and she had no damn bra under it. All that silver-blond hair was loose on her shoulders.

She looked like a fairy princess in some Disney movie—only better. Hotter, too.

She came straight for him, hips and breasts gently swaying. He clutched his second cup of coffee like a lifeline and told himself to turn away.

Didn't happen. She disappeared from sight as she mounted the short stairs to the deck. Behind him, Owen let out a happy little whine and padded straight for the slider.

Dante followed, reaching the glass door at the same time as Gracie did. For a moment they just stood there, staring at each other through the glass. Owen dropped to his haunches and whined up at Dante to open the door and let in the object of the mutt's complete adoration.

Very slowly, Gracie smiled. She lifted her right hand and pantomimed knocking without actually touching the glass.

"Stay," he commanded the dog.

Owen might be in love with Gracie Bravo, but he was a good dog and always obeyed a direct command. He stayed right where he was when Dante shoved the slider wide.

"Want some coffee?" At his feet, Owen quivered with eagerness, but he kept his butt to the floor.

"No, thanks. I just came to tell you dinner's at seven and you should be over at six—and yeah, I could have texted you. But what fun is that?"

"I'll be there." He stared straight into those fine blue eyes. It was a pleasure to do so and it also kept him from looking at her unconfined breasts.

"I'm roasting a chicken. Nothing fancy."

"Sounds good. I'll bring a bottle of white."

Owen was already over there when Dante arrived at six on the nose. Gracie was still wearing that silky, distracting cami.

But really, since last Tuesday night, everything about her distracted him. She could wear a burka and he would still spend every moment near her obsessing over what was under it.

He handed her the chilled bottle of wine and she carried it to the counter to open it.

"Smells good in here." He knelt to pet the dog, who greeted him by rolling over for a stomach scratch. "You've got bowls for him, too?" They were on the floor at the end of the counter. One was empty, the other had water in it.

"Have a seat at the table," she said as she popped the cork. "I never feed your dog, I promise."

He pulled out a chair and sat. "But I'll bet you have kibble."

"Well, just in case." She got down two wine-glasses and carried them and the opened bottle to the table, where she filled a glass and held it down to him.

He took it. "Thanks."

She claimed the chair opposite him, poured a glass for herself and sipped. "Yummy wine— and you know, I'm more than happy to watch him whenever I'm here."

That made him laugh. "You already watch him all the time."

"If you're here, it's not watching him. He's just coming over to visit, that's all."

He studied her face, wondering how it was that she always seemed to have a certain glow about her. "That's a distinction without a difference."

"Wrong. And the offer stands. Just let me know if you need me to look after him."

He glanced over at the dog, who lay on his back with his tongue hanging out. Dante prob-ably ought to put more effort into keeping him at home. But Owen was happy and Gracie liked hav-ing him around, so why mess with what seemed to be working out for everyone? "I think I'll just say I appreciate the offer and we should move on to some other, more interesting topic."

"Works for me."

They stared at each other. He wanted to touch her and knew that he wouldn't at the same time as he regretted saying they ought to talk about something more interesting.

Interesting topics could be dangerous—at that moment, *all* topics seemed off-limits. Anything they said could lead to an honest conversation. He might just blurt out something totally unacceptable, like how he couldn't stop thinking of her and he hadn't changed his sheets since the night she spent in them. They still smelled of her, though only faintly now. Of flowers. And sex.

She set her glass back on the table. "The chicken needs another half hour and then a little time to rest before we carve it. How 'bout a walk down to the beach?"

He set his glass next hers. "Let's go."

Owen led the way along the twisting, narrow path to the sand. This time of day, the beach was deserted. The lowering sun glittered on the water and the waves were slow and lazy, drifting in, sliding out.

They took off their shoes and strolled the shoreline, the dog running ahead and then doubling back to follow for a while, then taking off in front of them again.

It was nice, but too quiet. They were being careful with each other and he hated it. At the same time, he knew that saying anything too meaningful could lead somewhere he wasn't prepared to go.

They went to back to the cabin. She served the dinner. He tried not to stare at her sleek bare shoulders, at her thick, pale hair. At everything he wanted that he really needed *not* to let himself have.

Grace sat across from him at the small gateleg table and didn't really know where to go from here.

Tempting him until he broke didn't seem to be working. Plus, it was kind of childish. She realized that.

But the guy was impossible. They could have a great thing together if he'd only stop behaving like it was his sworn duty *not* to touch her ever again.

For once in her life, she was attracted to someone who didn't want her to fund his art or his writing or his next experiment. All Dante really wanted from her was companionship—and hot, sexy times, even if he refused to admit it.

He was the first traditional male who'd ever interested her in the least. And since the night they'd shared a bottle of great tequila and his bed, he interested her a whole lot. He was protective and considerate and smoking hot—when he wasn't being a damn idiot and turning her down.

After the meal, he helped her clear the table and volunteered to wash the dishes. It didn't take all that long.

He thanked her for the evening and said he had to go. She felt so disheartened, she didn't even try to stop him.

Maybe, really, she needed to simply accept that they'd shared one amazing night and it wasn't happening again.

For the rest of the week, she wore a bra when she hung around the cabin. She gardened in her oldest pair of baggy cargoes and she saw Dante only when she brought Owen back to him or waved at him because they both happened to be outside at the same time.

She figured she'd seriously messed up, lost a really good friend by getting naked with him. It was just another life lesson, she tried to tell herself. Constructive and depressing. Like blowing her inheritance supporting interesting men in Europe.

Some women never really worked it out, manwise. That didn't mean they couldn't have a rich and meaningful life. Look at the first Queen Elizabeth. They called her the virgin queen, though most reliable sources claimed the epithet was an exercise in irony. But whether she'd actually died a virgin or not, Elizabeth I never found a life partner. Yet she'd been the greatest ruler England ever had.

Time to face facts, Grace decided. She and Dante were over before they'd even really begun.

Chapter Four

That Saturday morning at ten, Dante arrived at the specified wide space in the road about midway between Valentine Bay and Portland to pick up his girls.

As always, he got there right on time.

And as usual, Marjorie and the girls were late. Dante played Fortnite on his phone and tried not to feel impatient as twenty minutes crawled by.

And then, finally, there they were, with Roger at the wheel of the white Toyota Sienna he'd owned before he and Marjorie got together. Because leave it to Roger Hoffenhower to drive a minivan even before he had a family to ferry around in it.

Roger pulled in behind Dante's Ram crew cab and Dante got out to help the girls move their mountains of belongings from the Toyota to the truck. Nic and Nat jumped out and came running as Marjorie called out the window, "Stay out of the road, you two!" They were on the passenger side of the minivan, nowhere near traffic, but Marjorie was a mother to the core.

His daughters squealed as he held out his arms. They landed against him, one on each side.

"Daddy!" cried Nicole as Natalie shrieked, "We're here!"

Had they grown since their last visit four weeks ago? Kind of seemed like it. They smelled of Sour Patch Kids and that all-natural mango-and-shea-butter shampoo Marj bought for them, and he forgot all about his annoyance at Roger for arriving late. It was everything in the world to him, just to have them in his arms.

For about a half a second.

Immediately, they were dropping to the ground again, whirling around to start grabbing their stuff, babbling on about their cousins and friends in Valentine Bay that they couldn't wait to see. They'd been coming to Dante every summer since they were three. It was pretty much the life they'd always known. They had friends, Marj's family and school in Portland and a whole other set of friends and family in Valentine Bay.

Roger got out and shook Dante's hand and they made friendly noises at each other for a minute or two as Marjorie tried to supervise getting the booster seats out of the minivan.

"We know how to get our seats," insisted Natalie.

"Yeah, Mom," moaned Nic. "We'd rather do it ourselves."

"Well, pardon me." Marj stepped back with both hands up.

The change-off went pretty smoothly, overall. And the girls weren't fighting or crying or complaining, so that was a win. Not ten minutes after Roger pulled in behind Dante, he and Marj were waving goodbye.

The girls buckled up in the back seat and off they went. The drive home took about an hour. Five minutes into the trip, they started working on him to stop at Camp 18 for burgers.

It wasn't even eleven yet. They could have sandwiches at the house.

But he was a single dad and he hadn't seen them for a month. Whatever they wanted, he wanted to give them.

And they knew it, too.

"Daddy, please?"

"Can we?"

"We *never* get to stop at Camp 18…"

They stopped at Camp 18. First came the pictures. He took a bunch of the two of them posing in front of various pieces of logging equipment on view out by the parking area. Then they started in on him about cell phones.

"We need our own phones, Daddy, we really do," insisted Nat as Nic stood beside her, nodding with enthusiasm. "If we had our own phones, we could take our *own* pictures…"

So far, he and Marj had held the line on the phone situation. The plan was to put off going there until the twins reached eighth grade. Yeah, he knew it was a losing battle, but at this point he and his ex were still presenting a united front on the issue. "We've talked about phones. A lot," he said patiently. "I don't think we need to go over all that again right now."

They aimed identical scowls at him.

But then Nic asked so sweetly, "Can we at least use your phone and take some pictures of each other?"

There went another half hour as they giggled and chattered together and took turns posing for each other in front of and on the giant chainsaw sculptures scattered around the series of porches leading into the log cabin–style restaurant and gift shop. Not that he minded them taking their time. They were having a ball and he had the weekend off and the plan was to spend it all with them, anyway.

When he finally herded them inside, they wanted to order everything on the menu. He just kept shaking his head until they narrowed it down to burgers with fries and lemon-lime sodas. The burgers were big, so he really tried to get them to split their order between them. But they looked at him through matching sets of wide brown, hopeful eyes and he was a goner. Food would be wasted.

But as it turned out, they were both hungry and really put it away. He was glad he'd let them have what they wanted. It was all going great—until Nic picked up her full soda just as Nat leaned close to her ear and whispered something.

Nic burst out laughing and stopped paying attention to the drink in her hand. The corner of her big plastic cup caught the edge of the table and sent ice and sticky soda raining into her lap, drenching her turquoise tank on the way, soaking her faded rolled-up jeans and even sliding down her calves to fill her pink-and-white-checked Vans.

She let out an outraged cry of surprise and stared down at the mess with a look of absolute horror.

And then Nat said in a gently chiding tone,

sounding just like their mother, "Nic, you really need to be more careful."

Nicole promptly burst into tears. "Oh, shut up, Nat," she sobbed. "You made me do it."

"Did not."

"Did so…"

The nice waitress came running with clean towels and gentle words. Dante was sent to the truck to get Nic some dry clothes as the waitress and Nat took the sobbing Nic to the restroom.

Of course, he brought back the wrong things.

"I'm not wearing those," Nicole moaned. He could hear every word clearly through the restroom door. "Nat, you have to go with him and show him what I need."

A moment later, Nat emerged carrying the clothes he'd brought from the pickup. "She's soaked all the way through," Nat said sternly. "And she's very upset." He must have looked pretty worried, because then she reassured him. "Come on, Daddy." She patted his arm. "It's going to be fine."

Back out to the truck they went. Nat dug around in one of Nic's suitcases, coming up with a top and some pants that, to him, looked pretty much like the ones he'd chosen in the first place. She also found clean underwear and another pair of canvas shoes.

They headed back to the restaurant and straight

to the restroom. He lurked near the door as his daughters spoke in whispers on the other side.

When they came out, he thought Nic looked pretty composed. She handed him a plastic bag provided by the waitress. "Here's my stuff," she said with distaste. "Everything's sticky."

"We'll dump them in the wash at home and they'll be good as new."

Though her tears had dried, her eyes were red from crying. "I know, Daddy. It's just *embarrassing*, that's all."

"Happens to everyone now and again."

She stuck out her lower lip with a tiny *humph* of sound and then added softly, "I'm sorry, Daddy."

"It was an accident." He dared to offer a hug and she accepted as Nat looked on approvingly.

"Ready to go home?" he asked them both, though as a rule with them he tried not to ask questions he might not like the answer to.

This time, though, he got the answer he was hoping for. Both of them nodded.

By nine that night when the girls went to bed, he was exhausted. He grabbed a quick shower and then checked on them. They were both sound asleep.

Grabbing a beer from the fridge, he went out to

sit on the deck, only realizing that Owen had escaped to Gracie's again when she emerged from the cabin with the dog right behind her. The light by the cabin door made a halo around her bright hair as she paused to pull it closed behind her.

He watched her coming toward him through the twilight, wearing jeans and a white T-shirt—with a bra underneath, he couldn't help but notice with more disappointment than he should have allowed himself to feel.

"Owen." He clicked his tongue and the dog loped up the deck steps and right to him. "Lie down."

Owen dropped to the deck boards and put his head on his paws. With a wave, Gracie started to turn back for the cabin.

He'd spent the whole day with a couple of eight-year-olds and he really couldn't help longing to look at a pretty woman, not to mention, talk to an adult. "Gracie."

She turned back to him again and braced her hands on her hips. "What'd I do now?"

"Want a beer?"

She tipped her head to the side, like she wasn't sure she ought to accept his invitation.

He got that. He'd been avoiding her and, judging by the bra she was now wearing and the disappearance of those revealing Daisy Dukes, she'd taken the hint.

"C'mon," he coaxed. "Just one." With a shrug, she came toward him. "Have a seat."

She dropped into the chair across from him and he got up and went in to get an IPA, handing it to her before he sat down again.

For a couple of minutes, they just sat there, sipping. He thought about how superfine she looked in the light by the slider behind him and couldn't help missing all that gorgeous skin she had hidden now under faded jeans and a plain shirt.

"Your daughters are adorable," she said.

He frowned at her. "You met them?"

She laughed. The sound tugged on something deep inside him, something that wasn't quite an emotion, something more basic. Something needful and hungry—and lonely, too. "I babysat them once, back when they were toddlers. It was here. At this house."

"I'd forgotten."

"They were a handful back then, but sweet. Kind of like Daniel's twins." She set the bottle down on the table, but didn't let go of it. "This afternoon, they came to the cabin to get Owen."

"Owen." At his feet, the dog lifted his head. Dante gave the dog a pat. "I should have known.

That must have been when I was trying to get their karaoke machine up and running. I had some trouble with the disco lights."

"But you got it working?" At his nod, she went on, "For identicals, I find them pretty easy to tell apart."

"Yeah, Nat's more athletic, more outgoing and opinionated. Nic is more in her own head, I guess you could say. She weighs maybe five pounds more than Nat, but she's pretty sensitive about it."

"They're both gorgeous."

"I couldn't agree more."

"Spoken like a really good dad."

He grinned at her across the table. "Hold that thought."

"Once you got the disco lights working, did they sing for you?"

"Let me put it this way. I don't really ever need to hear 'Let It Go' again."

Gracie ran a hand back through all that beautiful hair. What was it about her? Even in unrevealing clothes, she pretty much sucked the breath clean out of his lungs. She asked, "So they wore you out, huh?"

"They did. And I try to keep in shape, too. Valentine Bay is hardly a hotbed of crime, but I've taken down my share of bad actors and fleeing offenders.

None of them had half the energy of my two girls. Every time they come home, I realize all over again how nonstop they are. Always talking, on the move."

She was watching him. "I meant it when I said that you're a good dad, Dante."

"Thanks." He confessed, "I miss them so much when they're gone." Their eyes met and held. He never wanted to look away.

She was the one who broke the spell, slowly turning to stare off toward the shadows of the twisted trees that framed the path to the beach. "They're excited to be here. They told me they always do the day camp in Valentine City Park and have lots of friends they can't wait to see."

"Yeah. I get banker's hours when they're with me so I can work while they're at camp. Today, they were home for maybe two hours before they started begging to go to Grandma's. They can't wait to have sleepovers with their cousins and friends here in town. And they're already on me about where they can get the right costumes for the Medieval Faire—according to some all-knowing authority they somehow can't quite name, it's no good to just go to a discount store and pick up something simple and easy out of a box. It has to be 'special,' though neither of them seems that sure what 'special' involves."

Gracie turned those shining eyes on him again. "My sisters are running the Medieval Faire."

"Harper and Hailey?"

"Who else? They're the Barnum and Bailey of Valentine Bay, those two. I might be able to hook your girls up with what they need for the Faire. Harper's kind of a genius with costumes. She can take a bunch of random fabric and some rickrack and whip up something any medieval lady would be proud to wear."

He really wanted to kiss her. He wouldn't. Uh-uh. But he wanted to. Bad. It didn't matter in the least that she'd stopped running around braless in short shorts. Whatever she wore, he was interested. He would never forget their one night together and he kind of hated that it wasn't going to happen again.

"Dante?" She leaned toward him across the table. "Where'd you go?"

"I'm right here." It wouldn't take much to get his mouth on hers. He could lean in to meet her.

Not that she was necessarily interested anymore.

She sat back and picked up her beer again.

He ordered his brain to stay on task. "Getting two eight-year-olds the 'special' costumes they require is kind of a lot. I don't want to take advantage of you."

She let out a snort. "Oh, please. Look at all

you've done for me. I'm no longer living in my brother's house. Instead, I've got the perfect little cabin in a beautiful setting for five hundred a month, all because of you. Getting Nic and Nat costumes for the Faire is nothing, the least I can do. And it'll be fun, too."

Seeing her naked again, now *that* would be fun...

And what was the matter with him? He needed to get his mind out of the gutter.

He was hopeless when it came to her, no doubt about it.

Twin lines had formed between her smooth brows. "You okay, Dante? You seem kind of... I don't know. Sad, maybe. Or preoccupied."

There was nothing wrong with him that another night with her wouldn't cure—at least temporarily. Until the next night, when he would only be wanting her all over again.

"I'm fine," he lied. "'Nother beer?"

"Thanks, no." She set her empty bottle down and stood. "I need to change and head over to the Sea Breeze. Ingrid's short a bartender. She asked if I could make it in from eleven to closing—listen, tomorrow I'll reach out to my sisters about costumes for the girls."

"'Preciate it."

"I'll let you know."

He gave her a nod and then watched her walk away, feeling low that she was no longer sitting across from him.

Was he ridiculous? Damn straight.

Somehow, he needed to get over himself, either stop yearning for what he was never going to let himself have.

Or reach out and take it.

If she was still willing. If he hadn't already blown any chance he might have had with her.

During the family dinner at Daniel's the next day, Grace talked to Harper. She said she would love to put together costumes for Dante's twins. The Faire opened in two weeks. Harper said that was plenty of time to fix the twins up, as long as they got on it right away.

It wouldn't be right to get the twins' hopes up if Dante had changed his mind about Harper helping the girls out, so Gracie planned to wait until after nine when she knew the kids would be in bed to talk to him about it. She got home from Daniel's at a little past eight. It was weirdly nerve-racking, sitting in the cabin, waiting for the right time to go looking for him.

She'd been missing him. They *were* friends and

she hoped that someday they would get past what had happened on what she'd come to think of as the night of the tequila. She longed for them to be easy with each other again.

And okay, hard truth? Even with the current tension between them, she *liked* being alone with him. The way he looked at her caused small, fluttery creatures to buzz around in her belly in the best kind of way. Sometimes she even dared to imagine the day would come when he would admit that he ached to spend the night with her again.

Would she turn him down flat, as originally planned?

Better not to even think about what would happen if…

Dante was sitting on the deck with Owen when she went over there at ten past nine. With a nod at the chair across from him, he went in to get her a beer.

When he came back out, she explained that Harper would make the girls their costumes. "So we were thinking that on Tuesday, I could pick them up at the park after day camp and drive them over to the cottage where my sisters live. Harper will take measurements and sketch out what the finished dresses will look like. She says she can have them ready in a week or so."

"Sounds great. How much do I owe you and Harper?"

She gave him a serious eye-roll. "I told you last night. Nothing. I'm taking care of it."

"What does that mean?"

"It means my part of this is minimal. I'm taking the girls over there and bringing them home. And I already agreed with Harper on the price of the costumes. I'm paying that."

"No, you're not."

"This is ridiculous. Let it go, Dante."

He had on his bad-cop face, unreadable and harsh. "Okay, I'm willing to take advantage of *you*." She had to press her lips together to keep from making some silly, suggestive comment in response to that one. He went on, "Because you're so damn stubborn and I'm tired of arguing about it."

"Jeesh. Thanks?"

"But if Harper is making my girls their costumes, she's going to get paid for it by me."

They went back and forth a couple of times, Grace maintaining that she had it handled, Dante insisting she take his money, or else. In the end, she gave in and he went inside again, emerging a few minutes later with a check for her to give to Harper.

She reluctantly accepted the money and stood up to go.

"Sit back down," he commanded as he dropped into his chair. "Finish your damn beer."

She made a face at him. "Why? Because you're so much fun to be with?"

He gazed up at her through those fine dark eyes. His eyelashes were so thick and black. She wanted to reach out and touch them, feel them brush against her fingertips. She wanted to bend across the iron table between them and kiss that sexy mouth again, to have those big, muscular arms of his wrapping tight around her, pulling her in good and close to his heat and strength.

"Please." He said the word a little roughly. But kind of earnestly, too. Like he really, truly wanted her to stay.

When, exactly, did she become such a complete pushover for this man? The night of the tequila? Maybe.

More likely, it had started long before that, when he was always coming into the Sea Breeze and sitting at the bar, keeping her company while she worked. He would nurse a beer or two, maybe have sliders or fish tacos and fries. When things weren't too busy, they would talk. He was a good listener. Too serious, maybe. But the thing about

Dante was, he really did *care*—how a friend was doing, if everything was all right.

She sat down and picked up her half-finished beer. "Bad day?"

Dante set his beer down. "Tomorrow, I have to work. The girls will go to day camp."

She gave him a small shrug. "I'm aware of the schedule."

"All I mean is, two days into having them with me and I'm so ready to drop them off at City Park and spend the day reviewing arrest reports and conducting background investigations."

Gracie rested both forearms on the table and plunked her chin down on her folded hands. "You feel guilty, is that what you're saying?" She gave him a tiny smile and a hint of a dimple tucked itself into her left cheek.

He had a raging case of lust for her. And he liked her, too. So much. Too much?

Probably.

"Talk," she said.

"It's partly Roger," he grumbled.

"They use Roger against you?"

"Exactly. It's 'Roger lets us do this.' And 'Roger says we don't have to do *that*.' And 'Roger understands that we're eight and we need to have some independence—and lip gloss. Daddy, we're old enough for lip gloss.'"

Gracie laughed, a quiet little laugh, and sat back in her chair again. "I'm sure it's frustrating. But they really do seem like great kids. And it's natural for them to test boundaries and limits with you. Also, think about it—is there a kid alive who doesn't play one parent off against the other, at least a little?"

He couldn't stop himself from reminding her, "Roger isn't a parent. He's their stepdad."

"Oh, come on." She slanted him a look both ironic and reproachful. "Stepfathers count, too, in a child's life. And even you said he's a great guy. You're just jealous."

"Hey," he grumbled. "Whose friend are you, anyway?"

"Yours." She reached across and clasped his arm. It felt so good. Her palm was cool, her fingers soft. He wanted…

Never mind what you want, fool.

She took her hand away—too quickly, as though she'd caught herself doing something she shouldn't. He wanted to reach out and catch it, to lace his fingers with hers.

How bad did he have it for her, really?

Pretty damn bad. And it wasn't only that gorgeous face and rockin' body. She was good at heart and wise, too. Sometimes, when they talked, he forgot that she was almost a decade younger than him. He liked hearing whatever she had to say on any given subject.

"Be patient with them *and* with yourself," she advised.

"I'm working on it. I try to remember not to *always* draw the line on them, to be more permissive now and then. Being permissive isn't my strong suit, though."

"Really?" She poured on the sarcasm. "I never would have guessed…" But then she softened. "Honestly, though. They do seem happy and it's obvious they adore you."

He scoffed. "They think I'm a dinosaur who doesn't understand them the way Roger does."

She leaned in again. "They love you. You never have to doubt that. Show a little faith that they can love you and love Roger, too."

Tuesday, Gracie picked up Nicole and Natalie at the park after their day camp. They'd kept their booster seats that morning when Dante dropped them off and now, they hooked them up in the back seat of Grace's RAV4 themselves.

The two were bouncy and bright-eyed, going on about their best friends at camp and their first sleepover of the summer at their cousin Heather's house Saturday night.

"Aunt Lisa lets us stay up late," Natalie announced with glee.

"It's so much fun," Nicole chimed in. "They have a fire pit in back and we roast hot dogs and marshmallows for s'mores. Carly, our friend from camp, is coming, too."

A glance in the rearview mirror showed Grace that Natalie was nodding. "We can't hardly wait. We'll bring our sleeping bags and sleep outside and tell scary stories all night long."

At the rambling one-story cottage on a hill above the beach at the north end of town, Hailey whipped up strawberry smoothies. Harper had ten different costume sketches for the twins to choose from, each consisting of two layers. First, a long undertunic in a lightweight fabric. Then another, heavier tunic went on top. The overtunic designs, in damask and velvet, featured deep, strong colors. They were embellished with ornamental bands at the ends of the flowing sleeves, around the hem and dropped waist and at the neckline.

Harper had also provided a selection of wimple sketches so the girls could mix and match their headdresses with the gowns they chose. Grace, who'd studied medieval dress in college, had always considered the wimple to be about the ugliest thing a woman could wear on her head—no offense to all the excellent nuns the world over. However, the wimple was an authentic part of any medieval lady's wardrobe and Harper had done a beautiful job of sketching out various wimple styles. Gracie kept her opinion of that particular article of clothing to herself.

But then it turned out Natalie and Nicole felt the same. The two whispered together and then Natalie spoke up. "Can we skip this bandage thing on our heads?"

Harper had no problem with that. "Absolutely. Who needs a wimple, anyway? You should love what you wear or why bother?"

"I'm glad," declared Nat.

"We really love these dresses," added Nic.

Nat agreed. "It might take us a little while to choose…"

And it did. For more than an hour, they sipped their smoothies and ate apple slices and debated the strong points of this or that gown.

Grace took Harper aside as the girls pored over the different designs. "I planned to treat them to the dresses, but Dante wouldn't let me." She handed over the check.

"Whoa," said her sister. "This is more than I expected. Really, Gracie, I was only going to charge you for the fabric and notions."

"Cheap at the price. The girls are going to love those gowns and Dante was insistent that you should get paid for your work."

"Tell Dante thank-you."

"I will."

"How's it going, with the cabin and all?"

"I love it there."

Harper seemed to be studying her a little too closely. "But?"

"But nothing. It's a really cute place. Like this place, there's a private path down to the beach and the price is ridiculously low. Dante's a good, um, friend."

Harper looked at her sideways. "What's an 'um' friend?"

"That's a long story and I'm not tellin' it."

"Gracie." Harper reached out and stroked a hand down her arm. "I'm here. Hailey's here. For you."

It felt so good, just to hear her sister say that. Maybe she'd misjudged the situation with Hailey and Harper. Maybe feeling like an outsider around the two of them was more on her than on them.

The truth was, Grace had felt somewhat adrift lately, in terms of having other women she trusted to talk to. Her lifetime besties, Carrie and Erin, were still partying hearty all the time, ready for anything, while Grace was starting to be more about making a place for herself in life and succeeding at her chosen career. She'd kind of drifted away from them in the past year.

Now she was the one squeezing Harper's arm. "I appreciate the offer for some girl time. I really do. And I'll probably be taking you up on it one of these days."

"Anytime, the sooner the better. I mean that. We know Daniel used to be too hard on you."

"Well, we're okay now, Daniel and me. We really are."

"Good. He was always kind of grim about having all that responsibility dumped on his shoulders after Mom and Dad died."

"Yes, he was," Grace said with conviction.

"But then I kind of think it was also hard for him to let go of being a second dad to all of us. As the youngest, you had the toughest time getting him to see that you are all grown up."

Grace was kind of blown away at all this insight from her sister. "You are absolutely right."

"Just remember." Harper caught her hand and gave it a quick squeeze. "We've got another bedroom here and the price, for you, is even better than what you're paying Dante—I mean, you just can't beat free."

Somehow, Grace hadn't expected Harper or Hailey to be that thrilled at the idea of her moving in on them. Apparently, she'd been wrong about that, too. Which had her throat going tight and her eyes turning misty. "Thank you."

"Nothing to thank me for. This house is for anyone in the family who needs it. And Hailey and I would love to have you here."

Grace didn't know what to say. She pulled her sister into a quick, tight hug. "It means a lot—you know, to have the option."

"Anytime." Harper whispered, "And I gotta ask. You and Dante? Maybe?"

"Like I said, we're friends." The words tasted sour in her mouth.

Harper was grinning—and still whispering. "No doubt about it now. I'm picking up an undercurrent, hot goings-on with a hot cop. You need to talk about it. With me."

"Uh-uh. Not happening."

"Shake your head all you want," said her sister. "I'm not convinced. You've got to come over some evening, and tell all—or tell nothing if that's how you want it. But come over and spend some time with us, please."

Grace promised that she would.

When Nat and Nic had finally made their choices, Harper took their measurements and said she expected them back for a final fitting a week from today. Then she would make any necessary alterations and the dresses would be ready that following Friday, the day before the Faire opened.

Dante had chicken cooking on the grill when Gracie brought the twins home at a little after seven.

She pulled in at the front gate and the girls got out, unhooked their booster seats and carried them into the garage.

He called to Gracie from the top step, "Barbecued chicken? I've got plenty."

She leaned across the seat and hollered out the open passenger window. "Can't. I'm closing at the Sea Breeze. Gotta be there by eight. Rain check?"

Disappointment he shouldn't be feeling twisted inside him, but he tried not to show it. "You got it."

"Harper says thank-you for the check."

"Worth every penny," he replied with a friendly wave—because that's what they were. Friends.

She waved back and drove off around the house on her way to the cabin. He went inside and on out back to the deck, where he turned the chicken over and then called the girls to set the table.

While they ate, the twins talked nonstop about the costumes Harper Bravo was making for them and the fun they'd had that afternoon with the beautiful, grown-up Bravo sisters.

"Grace is the best," declared Nat. "She's almost like another kid, a really nice kid, and smart. A kid who *knows* stuff, someone you can talk to."

"Talk to about what?" asked Dante.

Both girls frowned at him. Finally, Nat answered, "Everything," and went right on talking before he could try to get some specifics out of her. "Hailey made us smoothies."

"They were *so* good." Nic beamed.

"Strawberry," Nat said. "We had the smoothies while we picked which costumes we wanted. Mine will be gold underneath with red velvet on top and lots of gold trim."

"And mine's green," said Nic, "and kind of silvery underneath, with silver trim. Harper drew these beautiful pictures of the dresses she could make for us. It was really hard to choose which one."

"And it took a long time, too," Nat added, eyes going wide.

"But it was worth it," said Nic.

"*So* worth it," Nat agreed. "We have to go back next Tuesday…" She paused to sip her milk.

"For a final fitting," Nic finished for her as Nat carefully set down her glass.

The girls chattered on. Dante got the memo, loud and clear. In bold, all caps. His kids and his dog couldn't get enough of the gorgeous, generous, big-hearted woman he kept telling himself he couldn't have sex with again. Ever.

Because he was too old for her and he didn't do actual relationships. He was no damn good at them, a complete slacker in the love department. The only one in his family who'd been born without the talent for being in love and staying that way. And let us not forget that Connor would probably knock his teeth down his throat if he ever found out what had happened between Dante and Connor's baby sister.

Dante wished she'd come over for dinner. But it was probably better she hadn't. Keeping his hands off her was an exercise in constant diligence. He could break at any time.

It was getting to the point where he kind of couldn't wait to break.

And that was wrong. So wrong. He should be avoiding her, not trying to lure her to the deck nightly with barbecued chicken and beers. Yet, as each day went by, he grew less certain of all the very good reasons he really needed to keep his greedy hands to himself.

"Daddy," said Nat, clearly perturbed.

"Huh?"

"You aren't listening," Nic chided.

"We're telling you all this important stuff." Nat set down a chicken bone and wiped her hands on her napkin. "And you're just sitting there looking like this." Nat let her mouth drop open and put on a vacant stare.

"Oh, come on. I'm not *that* bad."

Nic reached over and patted his arm with her soft little hand. "You need to pay some contentions, Daddy," she instructed in a gentle tone.

"You mean 'attention,' that I need to pay *attention*." Now and then, the girls still got the bigger words turned around.

Nic looked puzzled—but only for a second or two. "Yeah. That. It's important."

He promised them he would do better. They resumed their endless chatter and he did his best to listen to every word they said and not to let his mind wander to dangerous thoughts of Gracie Bravo.

Chapter Five

Saturday around six, Dante arrived home from dropping the twins off at his brother's for a sleepover. Owen was waiting just inside the front door when he entered the house. The dog looked up at him pleadingly.

"Walk?" he asked. At Owen's eager whine, he grabbed the leash he rarely used and a baggie for cleanup and took the dog out the back slider for a run down on the beach.

Gracie's ancient Toyota was parked in the graveled parking spot on one side of the cabin. Light shone through the windows on either side of the door. He could see her at the kitchen counter in there.

"Hey!" he called as he went by.

"Hey!" she answered from inside.

A moment later, she opened the door. He drank in the sight of her, in a tank top—with a bra under it, damn it—and shorts that were unfortunately *not* those magical Daisy Dukes he so fervently admired. She had all that silver-blond hair corralled in two pigtails. He tried really hard not to imagine wrapping them around his fist from behind, giving them a good, hard tug so she tipped her head back and gave him her mouth for a deep, wet kiss.

She asked, "What's up?" Owen detoured to the front step and plunked to his butt in front of her. "Hello, handsome." She knelt to properly show her affection and he wished he was Owen, getting a scratch around the neck, being allowed to lick her face.

"Just a walk down to the beach." He shouldn't ask. But then he couldn't stop himself. "You working tonight?"

"I'm off." She rose to her feet again and Owen trotted back to his side. "And on a Saturday, no less. I traded with one of the other bartenders. I had the Fourth off and she really wanted it—family coming into town, she said."

His next question? Yeah, pretty much inevitable. "So what are you up to?"

"Just hanging at home, taking it easy."

"I've got some steaks and baby potatoes. I'll be firing up the grill as soon as Owen and I get in a quick run along the beach. Join me for dinner?"

For a moment, she just looked at him, those jewel-blue eyes unreadable. He braced himself for a no. But then she said, "Nicole and Natalie are at their cousin's tonight, right?"

"That's right. First sleepover of the summer."

"They mentioned it the other day."

"It's a very big deal," he said. "Momentous, even."

"Yeah, I heard rumors of untold delights. Hot dogs. S'mores. Scary stories all night long…"

"Don't tell me the details. I'll only worry they're eating too much junk food and not getting enough sleep."

"They're going to have a wonderful time." She said it kind of tenderly, like he needed reassurance that his girls were all right and sleepovers were an important part of an eight-year-old's social life. At his side, Owen was eager to be moving on. The dog whimpered with impatience as Dante and the gorgeous creature in the cabin doorway stood silently gazing at each other. And then she said, "I'll bring a salad and a bottle of red."

After dinner on the deck, they cleared the table and came back outside to watch the sun sink below the water way out on the ocean. The bottle of wine was still more than half-full. They were both being careful this time not to drink too much.

Something about her made him start blabbing stuff he never told anyone. Like how he and Marjorie were essentially broken up when she found out she was pregnant.

Grace didn't seem the least surprised at the news. "So you decided to try again?"

He studied her face and realized he would never get tired of looking at her. "Somebody already told you that Marjorie was pregnant when we got married, right?"

She gave him the barest hint of a smile. "Women talk. You need to get used to it."

"Must've been my sister. When did you have time to talk to Aly about me?"

She only tipped her head to the side, causing one of those sexy pigtails to swing down along the silky skin of her bare arm. The damn pigtail seemed to be taunting him, tempting him to reach across and give it a tug.

He dragged his gaze back up and focused on meeting her eyes. "You're not going to tell me if it was Aly, are you?"

"Nope."

Did he care that much who'd told her? Not really. He let it go and went back to saying more than he should about what went down with him and his ex-wife. "Marjorie had moved here to be with me after college, but she missed her family and friends in Portland. It wasn't working out for either of us, really. We broke up and she moved home—and then she found out she was pregnant. I asked her to marry me. She came back to Valentine Bay. The girls were born. We lasted as a couple until they were two and then Marjorie said she just couldn't do it anymore. She said that she and I were over and we needed to accept that."

"So...she filed for divorce and returned to Portland?"

"Yeah. The rest is history. At least, it should've been."

"Except...?"

"For the next three years or so after Marj and I called it quits, I remained fake married to her anyway."

"What does 'fake married' mean?"

"It means I couldn't let go. If I had a day off and the girls were with her, I drove to Portland to check on her and see my daughters. While I was there, I would fix stuff around Marj's house, change the oil in her car, whatever she needed."

"You wanted to get back together with her?"

"I wanted to be a family with my girls and their mother."

"You're saying you felt that you and Marjorie *should* get back together?"

"That's it. That's right. Eventually, Marj drew the line on me. She said we weren't married and we would never be married again and I had to stop appearing at her doorstep, coming to her rescue all the time. It wasn't good for either of us, she said—and it wasn't fair to our daughters because it was too confusing for them. She said we had to face reality. It was over and it had been over for a long time."

Gracie smoothed both of her braids forward over her shoulders and held on to the ends of them. She looked so young, tugging on her pigtails, one sleek bare leg crossed over the other one. "Were you still in love with her?" she asked.

"No." Sometimes he doubted that he'd ever been in love with Marjorie. "I just wanted to make it work. I really did. For the girls' sake. And because Marj is a good woman. Because making it work is the right thing to do."

"I have to ask." Gracie wrinkled her nose and stared off into space.

"Go ahead."

She turned those unforgettable eyes on him again. "Are you saying you didn't have sex with anyone for three years, while you were driving back and forth to Portland to fix your ex-wife's... whatever?"

He shouldn't be talking about sex with her. He shouldn't be talking about his failed marriage or the wife he'd never loved the way a man should.

And yet, once again, he laid it right out there. "For about a year after Marjorie moved back to Portland, she and I would hook up occasionally. Then she told me she wouldn't sleep with me again and she was going to see other guys. I was so pissed off about that. There I was, knocking myself out to get us back together and she just announces she wants to go out with other men. I hit the roof, said things I shouldn't have. Marj never raised her voice. She just held firm. She was moving on. So, I started seeing other women. I'm no monk, for God's sake. I've just learned my lesson when it comes to love and marriage and forever after. I'm not cut out for that. I'm not looking for anything serious and I'm not getting married again and I make that very clear to any woman I spend time with."

"I see." She let go of her braids and recrossed those beautiful legs.

His mouth was dry and he ached to kiss her—to do a lot more than kiss her, if he was honest about it. "I'm sorry. You didn't need to hear all that."

"Didn't I?" Those deep blue eyes of hers seemed

to look right inside his head, to know every hot, sexy thought he kept trying really hard not to have about her. Sometimes she made him feel that *he* was too young for *her*. Another of those mysterious smiles curved her plump lips. "I've got a few things to tell *you*, too."

He grabbed his wine and knocked back a big gulp of it. "Why am I nervous, all of a sudden?"

She giggled then, and suddenly she was once more the young, carefree Gracie, ready for fun, up for anything. "The morning after we shared that bottle of tequila and ended up in bed together, when you said we could never do it again…?"

He realized he was holding his breath and let it out carefully. "Yeah?"

"I decided to torment you, to punish the crap out of you. My plan was to drive you insane with desire and then, when you finally begged me for one more night, to turn you down flat."

He liked her so much. Liked everything about her. Liked her enough that it kind of freaked him out. Maybe. A little. "You've been a very bad girl."

She snickered. "Oh, yes, I have." Her expression grew more serious. "Or I was. But then I kind of decided I was being childish. I put the short shorts away and put on a bra."

"Gracie?" He really needed to watch himself or he'd be saying what he shouldn't say.

"Hmm?"

That stuff he shouldn't say? He said it anyway. "Bra or no bra, your plan worked."

She uncrossed those spectacular legs and leaned into him. "Is this it, then?" It came out breathless and her eyes were softer, the pupils dilated. He ached to reach for her. She asked again. "Is this the moment you break?"

It was. Absolutely. "Yeah. You might as well go ahead and tell me right now to forget it."

She looked…stricken suddenly, every last trace of that breezy seductiveness gone.

The wounded look in her eyes kind of freaked him out. "Gracie. What's wrong?"

"Who am I kidding? I won't say no. I want you, too, Dante. Way too much to turn you down."

Chapter Six

Am I a complete fool? Gracie wondered.

Yeah. Probably.

Didn't matter. There might not be a tomorrow for her and Dante. But sometimes right now can be a very fine thing.

She got up and held down her hand to him. He took it without the slightest hesitation. A dark, heated shiver skated up her arm from just the touch of his fingers on her skin.

"Come here." He rose and pulled her around the small table until she stood in front of him. Only then did he release her—to clasp her by the waist.

"You're so beautiful." His mouth swooped down. "God, I missed having my hands on you."

She lifted up.

And finally, after far too many days and nights, they were kissing again. His mouth tasted of wine and the gelato they'd had for dessert. She'd missed him, too. So much.

His big, broad hands skated up her torso and she lifted her arms to wrap them around his neck. He smelled so good, like cedar and cloves and sheer, burning need.

She broke the kiss.

He opened his eyes. She saw such yearning in his face and found herself thinking that he didn't really understand how deeply he cared. He denied the power of his own emotions, seemed to take a dark kind of pride in being tough and calm and always in control of himself.

"Self-denial," she said. "It's kind of a thing with you."

"Not tonight, it isn't." He growled the words— and then he narrowed those midnight-dark eyes at her. His sensual mouth turned down. "Wait. Did you just change your mind?"

She reached up and framed his face with her hands. His cheeks were smooth now, though he'd been sporting some serious five o'clock shadow when he stopped by the cabin earlier to ask her over for dinner. He'd shaved for her. She didn't mind a little beard scruff. But she loved that he must have had some hope they might end up in each other's arms tonight, that he wanted to be smooth shaven for her.

Oh, she couldn't wait to kiss him some more, to touch him all over, to memorize again every muscled ridge, every dip and hollow. His body ran hot. She wanted to press herself tightly against him, to melt into him until there was nothing between them but the hunger and the pleasure they stirred in each other.

Until the only reality was the two of them moving together, naked and shameless, all through the night.

"No," she said, her voice soft, her intention firm. "I haven't changed my mind. No way. I want to be with you tonight." She surged up and took his mouth.

That kiss lasted longer than the first one, until she felt boneless. Liquid. Breathless, too.

"Let's go inside." He caught her earlobe between his teeth and gave it a tug.

She moaned and pushed away enough to see his eyes. They were dark as onyx, heavy lidded with arousal. "The cabin," she said. "*My* place this time." If he got freaked out like before and wanted to escape her in the morning, he could just go. She wouldn't have to suffer through the awfulness of him trying to get rid of her.

"However you want it."

She gave a low laugh then. "Now you're talkin'. Grab my salad bowl, lock up and let's go."

In the cabin, they pulled down the shades.

"Leave the lights on," he commanded.

"Works for me."

He pointed to the dog bed over by the fireplace. She'd bought it last week so Owen would have his own spot in her living space. "Go lie down." The dog trotted right over there and made himself comfortable. Then Dante turned those dark eyes on her. "Come here."

He caught her hand. She stepped out of her flip-flops and into his arms. His mouth came down to claim hers in a scorching kiss.

"Everything off." He breathed the command against her parted lips. But when she tried to un-button her shorts, he made a growling sound and pushed her hands away. "Uh-uh. I'll do it."

"So controlling…"

A low, rough chuckle escaped him. He kissed her slow and deep as he set about undressing her. Tugging the zipper wide on her shorts, he shoved them down, taking her panties right along with them. Those panties were a favorite of hers. Cheekies in cherry-red lace.

They fell unnoticed to the rag rug along with her shorts. And then his big hand was sliding between her legs. An approving growl escaped him as he stroked her wetness.

"Beautiful," he muttered thickly. "Perfect." He grabbed the globes of her bottom and pulled her up to him, hard and tight, so she could feel how much he was enjoying this. His big fingers digging into her backside, he licked and bit his way over her jaw and down the side of her throat. "This, too." He had the hem of her top in his hands and was already pulling it up. "It has to go." His voice rumbled against her collarbone.

She simply lifted her arms and he took it away, leaving her standing in front of him in only her red lace bra and two pink hair elastics, one at the end of each braid. When she reached up to pull off one of the elastics, he caught her hand.

"Leave the braids. I like them." His eyes promised things—lovely, sexy things. She sighed and dropped her hand.

He was gazing at her red bra now. "Pretty." Lifting a finger, he traced the lace of one cup,

"One Minute" Survey

You get up to **FOUR** books <u>and</u> TWO Mystery Gifts...

ABSOLUTELY FREE!

See inside for details.

YOU pick your books –
WE pay for everything.
You get up to FOUR new books and TWO Mystery Gifts..
absolutely FREE!
Total retail value: Over $20!

Dear Reader,

Your opinions are important to us. So if you'll participate in our fast and free "One Minute" Survey, **YOU** can pick up to four wonderful books that **WE** pay for!

As a leading publisher of women's fiction, we'd love to hear from you. That's why we promise to reward you for completing our survey.

IMPORTANT: Please complete the survey and return it. We'll send your Free Books and Free Mystery Gifts right away. **And we pay for shipping and handling too!** *We pay for EVERYTHING!*

Try **Harlequin® Special Edition** books featuring comfort and strength from the support of loved ones and enjoying the journey no matter what life throws your way.

Try **Harlequin® Heartwarming™ Larger-Print** books featuring uplifting stories where the bonds of friendship, family and community unite.

Or TRY BOTH!

Thank you again for participating in our "One Minute" Survey. It really takes just a minute (or less) to complete the survey… and your free books and gifts will be well worth it!

Sincerely,
Pam Powers

Pam Powers
for Reader Service

www.ReaderService.com

"One Minute" Survey

GET YOUR FREE BOOKS AND FREE GIFTS!

✓ Complete this Survey   ✓ Return this survey

▼ DETACH AND MAIL CARD TODAY! ▼

1 Do you try to find time to read every day?
☐ YES ☐ NO

2 Do you prefer stories with happy endings?
☐ YES ☐ NO

3 Do you enjoy having books delivered to your home?
☐ YES ☐ NO

4 Do you find a Larger Print size easier on your eyes?
☐ YES ☐ NO

YES! I have completed the above "One Minute" Survey. Please send me my Free Books and Free Mystery Gifts (worth over $20 retail). I understand that I am under no obligation to buy anything, as explained on the back of this card.

☐ I prefer Harlequin®
Special Edition
235/335 HDL GNXG

☐ I prefer Harlequin
Heartwarming® Larger Print
161/361 HDL GNXG

☐ I prefer BOTH
235/335 & 161/361
HDL GNMT

FIRST NAME   LAST NAME

ADDRESS

APT.#   CITY

STATE/PROV.   ZIP/POSTAL CODE

Offer limited to one per household and not applicable to series that subscriber is currently receiving.
Your Privacy—The Reader Service is committed to protecting your privacy. Our Privacy Policy is available online at www.ReaderService.com or upon request from the Reader Service. We make a portion of our mailing list available to reputable third parties that offer products we believe may interest you. If you prefer that we not exchange your name with third parties, or if you wish to clarify or modify your communication preferences, please visit us at www.ReaderService.com/consumerschoice or write to us at Reader Service Preference Service, P.O. Box 9062, Buffalo, NY 14240-9062. Include your complete name and address.

SE/HW-520-OM20

© 2019 HARLEQUIN ENTERPRISES ULC
™ and ® are trademarks owned by Harlequin Enterprises ULC. Printed in the U.S.A.

following it across the top slope of her breast, then moving on to the other one, drawing a sweet cascade of goose bumps along her skin, making her nipples go hard and tight. "Let me see…" He tugged on the lace, pulling it down, using his other hand to lift her breast up and push the lace below it. He did the same with the other cup, creating quite the display.

"You know, I'm all but naked with my boobs sticking out," she remarked, trying her best not to sound as breathless and needy as she felt. "And you're still wearing all your clothes."

"No complaining." He actually had the nerve to shake a finger at her. "I'm busy here." He bent close then and took her nipple in his mouth. She tried not to groan at the stab of sheer pleasure as his teeth closed around the hardened nub and he started to suck.

"You are so bad," she whispered, gathering him even closer, spearing her fingers in his thick, wavy hair, breathing in the heat and the dizzying scent of him. "Just a bad, bad man."

He kissed the tight flesh over her breastbone as he moved on to the other nipple, biting a little as he drew on it. It felt so good, painful in the most delicious way. And his hands weren't idle. They played her below. She could feel his erection, full and hard, against her hip.

When he lifted his head and looked in her eyes again, he said, "Get on the bed."

She might have talked back to him, just to let him know he wasn't the boss of her. But then again, what was there to argue about, really? Getting prone on the bed seemed like an excellent idea to her. She climbed up and stretched out with her head on the pillows. "Now what, oh lord and master?"

He watched her, his eyes dark fire, burning her, searing right down to the core of her, as he emptied his pockets, setting three condoms, his keys and his phone on the nightstand. Then he undressed, turning first to sit on the edge of the mattress and get rid of his boots and socks, then rising to peel everything else away.

She got to watch. It took him only a minute to strip himself bare, but it was a terrific minute. She drank in the sight of his broad, muscled shoulders and big arms, his deep chest and flat belly with its perfect trail of silky black hair leading down to the ready evidence that he really, really liked her. Every bit of him was just right. Just as she remembered from that first night.

Even drunk as she'd been, she did remember. All of it. The sheer glory of it.

And it was even better now, with her senses completely awake and attuned to him. Whatever happened in the morning, she would have tonight.

He came down to her.

And then he kissed her.

Time kind of flew away. There were only his strong arms around her, his mouth claiming hers in a long, thorough kiss before he moved down her body, settled between her thighs and guided her legs up over his shoulders.

"The taste of you…" He spoke the words against her core, rough and low and hungry. "I remember, Gracie. I remember everything. I won't ever, ever forget…"

"Good," she replied. "So, so very good…" And it was. The best. Even better than the time before. "Yes. Oh, absolutely. Beyond the faintest shadow of a doubt… Yes!" She speared her fingers into his hair, braced her heels on his hard shoulders and opened her legs even wider. Lifting her hips eagerly, she pressed her eager body up into his wonderful kiss.

She could lie there forever, moaning and writh- ing, with his mouth making magic, his fingers driving her crazy, curling inside her, finding that perfect spot that sent her straight to the moon.

How did he do it? How did he know just how to touch her, how to kiss her, how to drive her happily out of her mind? It really was not fair that he was so good at this. Not fair in the least.

And oh, please, if only he might never, ever stop...

Too quickly, she was flying over the moon and straight to the stars. She pulled on his hair and yanked him harder against her as she moaned out her climax and cried his name.

When she finally went lax, he prowled up her body, dropping a chain of kisses along the way, finally taking her mouth, slow and so sweet. She laughed against his lips, pressing her hands to his cheeks to rub her own wetness away.

"You're much too good at that," she scolded.

"I live to serve." He caught her lower lip between his teeth and tugged, stretching it deliciously before letting it pop free.

With a snort of affectionate derision, she shoved at his shoulders. She couldn't wait to give him a big dose of his own medicine.

But he was already reaching toward the nightstand, grabbing a condom.

"Give me that." She snatched it from him.

And for once, he let her have her way. She took it out of the wrapper, pushed him over onto his back and straddled him.

"Who's bossy now?" That sinful mouth of his curved in a lazy smile and his gaze roamed over her, possessive and so hot. He reached up and cupped her breasts, which were still in their cradle of lace. Using his thumbs, he idly flicked at her nipples. "You wreck me, Gracie. You blow me away."

She sighed in sheer pleasure, at the feel of his hands on her flesh and also at the rough, needful sound of his voice. For a moment, she just sat there on top of him, staring into his eyes, wishing...

But no.

There was now, tonight, and it was just beautiful. But he showed zero inclination to get over his conviction that he wasn't cut out for a lasting relationship.

No need to go wanting something she would never have.

Better to fully enjoy what was offered and let the future take care of itself. Really, she'd always been good at both.

Those big hands slid around to her back and he unclasped her bra. One at a time, he guided the straps down her arms. Still holding the unused condom, she stretched out her arms so he could take the bra away. "There," he said, his hands back beneath her breasts again and then trailing down her torso. Gently, he grasped her hips. "Well?"

"I'm on it." She rolled the condom down over his thick, hard length, easing it all the way to the base, taking care not to tear it as she worked. Once she had it in place, she lifted up to her knees and guided him to her. Slowly, she sank down on him, letting her head fall back. A luxurious groan escaped her as he filled her.

He groaned, too.

She looked down into those ebony eyes and they shared a smile. Then he reached up and took hold of both of her braids and slowly pulled her down until her lips met his.

He took her face between his hands. "You are spectacular. I never want to let you go."

Then don't, she thought. But all she said was, "Feels so good…"

She began to move, lifting and lowering, rolling against him, loving the feel of him, so thick and hot, deep and then deeper, so perfect. Just right.

He clasped her hips again, pulling her down tight, then letting her rise—only to drag her close once again.

She moaned in delighted surprise when he flipped her over and took the top position. Kneeling up, his hands still holding her hips, he pulled her lower body with him and guided her legs over his shoulders. By then, she was flying.

"So close," she whispered. "I'm almost..." A soft cry of pleasure escaped her.

"Now," he commanded as he surged deep within her.

And that did it. Her climax opened her up, spilling a shimmer of purest sensation. Starting at the core of her, the pleasure radiated outward in glorious waves. As she reached the peak, she felt him begin to pulse deep within her.

"Going," he groaned at her.

"Gone," she moaned back.

She woke to someone whining.

Carefully opening one eye, she found it was daylight and she was nose to nose with Owen, breathing in his doggy breath. "You need a mint," she grumbled.

A sleepy voice behind her said, "He wants to go out." Dante lifted his arm from its spot in the curve of her waist and tugged on one of her braids. She turned her head back to him and he kissed her, a sweet, chaste brush of his lips across hers.

Then he was rolling away from her, getting out on the other side of the bed. "I'll take him."

She braced up an elbow and watched Dante pull on his jeans. He zipped up and then dropped back to the mattress to put on his socks and lace up his Timberlands. When he stood again, he raked his hands back through his hair to kind of minimize the bedhead. Actually, he looked downright delicious, all rumpled and manly, with those muscles everywhere.

And she had no doubt at all that her braids were a mess, her hair sticking out every which way, with last night's mascara smeared where it shouldn't be.

"Be right back," he promised.

She realized she'd kind of been expecting him to start making excuses, acting all apologetic, saying he had to get going. But no. He was coming back. That pleased her no end. She couldn't stop herself from beaming him a huge, happy smile. "I'll make the coffee."

"Deal." Pulling open the door, he clicked his tongue. "Owen. Come." The dog went out and Dante followed.

As soon as he was gone, she jumped up and ran to the bathroom, where she rinsed away her raccoon eyes, combed her hair and brushed her teeth.

She had her clothes back on and was spooning grounds into the coffee maker when Dante and Owen returned. The dog went to his water bowl.

Dante came up behind her, wrapped his arms around her and kissed her neck. It felt really good. Also, domestic. Like they were a real couple.

Down, girl, she ordered her romantic heart. *It's a kiss on the neck, not a promise of forever.*

Not that she would want forever anyway. She had a lot to do in her life and she didn't need some man to make it all worthwhile.

However, the *right* man would be nice. One of these days. When the stars finally aligned.

Dante bit her earlobe. It felt so good. "You took out the braids. I really liked those braids."

She laughed, pushed the button to start the brew cycle, and slithered around to face him. "You like to pull on them."

He put up both hands. "Shoot me. I like to pull on them a lot."

"Be nice to me. You might see those braids again."

"Whatever it takes." His eyes had that smoldering look she very much enjoyed.

Did that mean last night was more than a one-time thing? She would really like that. Maybe too much. "You want some eggs?"

"I do. Got bacon?" He arched a thick, dark eyebrow at her.

"Yes, I have bacon." Owen sat at their feet staring up at them hopefully. "Kibble's in the bottom right cupboard if you want to pour him some."

Dante waited until after they'd eaten to bring up the elephant in the room. He poured them both more coffee first.

When he sat back down, he took a slow sip and said, "I'm through lying to myself about you and me, Gracie. I want more. Of you. Of this."

She stared across the battered old table at him. *More of Dante.* The prospect excited her. And scared her, too. What if she came to care too much? What if she already did? Cautiously, she asked, "So…what are you thinking?"

He looked down at the table, then dragged his gaze back up to meet hers. "Could it be just between us? Just you and me? I don't want the families to know. We would never hear the end of it. And I have no idea how Connor might react."

"I do not get what Connor has to say about it."

"We have history, me and Connor. You know that."

"Come on, it's none of Connor's business what you and I do in our own private lives."

"Yeah, well. Connor might think otherwise."

She put up both hands. "Fine. Whatever. The families won't know. Can we move on?"

He looked as relieved as she felt. "Absolutely."

"So you're saying a secret fling?" And actually, given that what they had wasn't really going anywhere, keeping it just between the two of them wasn't such a bad idea.

"I really like you, Gracie. And I want you. So damn much. I'm through pretending I can keep my hands off you. I want to be with you, but I'm still the same guy and I'm not going to change."

She dropped her head back and groaned at the ceiling. "Just answer the question."

"Yeah. A secret fling."

"What about seeing other people?"

That had him leaning in again, his face turned hard and dark. "No way. Just you and me. For as long as it lasts. No one else. For either of us."

"Not real big on sharing, huh?"

He looked almost hurt. "You are?"

"No." She gave him a slow grin. "But I sure do like yanking your chain."

He studied her for several endless seconds. "Okay, then. You and me. Nobody else and nobody knows."

"Until one of us calls a halt?"

"Yeah."

She thought of his daughters. "As long as the girls are here, we're not going to have a lot of chances to be together."

He reached across the table, as though to take her hand. But then he pulled back without touching her. He picked up his cup and drank. "Not exactly an irresistible offer, is it? Just tell me to shove it."

She walked her fingers to the middle of the table, turned her hand over and waited, palm up.

It took him a minute, but he put his mug down and covered her hand with his. It felt wonderful. Right. To have his hand wrapped around hers.

She said, "So then, what with keeping it secret and the girls living with you, we won't be spending all that many nights together. It's my considered opinion that we need to make the most of every moment we get."

All of a sudden, his dark eyes seemed to shine with the brightest light. Still holding her hand, he got up. She rose at the same time. It took only a tug on her hand and she was in his arms.

He wrapped her up tight and kissed her slow and deep. When he lifted his head, he asked in a rough whisper, "Did you just say yes?"

"Yes, Dante. Yes."

Chapter Seven

Dante was more than happy to seek out opportunities to be alone with Gracie.

He rarely drove home for lunch. But the next day, Monday, he took a flyer on the off chance that Gracie might be there.

She was. He spotted her little SUV parked beside the cabin and drove the cruiser on back there. Wearing those dinky shorts he so greatly admired and a T-shirt with History Buff printed on it beneath a flexing bodybuilder, she was waiting in the open doorway for him when he sprinted up the pebbled walkway.

She laughed and wrapped her arms around his

neck as he scooped her high against his VBPD blues. "I do believe I'm about to experience my first luncher," she said.

"Nooner," he corrected, nuzzling her neck.

"Oh, Officer." She heaved an over-the-top sigh. "Whatever you call it, I need it. Now…"

And he got to spend forty-five minutes in the cabin with Gracie, naked. Those minutes raced by. He relished every one of them.

Monday night, after the girls were in bed, he texted her and she came over. They had a beer on the deck and compared daytime schedules. Her hours at the bar changed every week and he sometimes got stuck at the station house or out working a case and had to skip lunch. They agreed it would be easier if he just called or texted when he could get away in the daytime. That way he wouldn't waste his time driving home if she couldn't meet him there.

When she got up to go, he grabbed her hand and pulled her down onto his lap. "Don't leave. Not yet." He kissed her.

Eventually, he had to let her mouth go. She said, "I have to be at work at…"

He kissed her again before she could finish. "There isn't enough time for us."

She nipped at his earlobe. "It's a secret fling.

Deal with it." Her voice was light and teasing, while he felt all dark and twisted inside, full of needs he really didn't want to address.

He wanted her. Constantly.

And he was going to have to lighten up and count his damn blessings. At least now, for as long as it lasted, he could have her whenever their schedules lined up.

It just wasn't often enough. Not by a long shot.

"Dante…" She said his name in a sweet little singsong. And then she kissed the side of his throat. "I really do have to go." He stole one more kiss and somehow kept himself from grabbing for her when she rose from his lap, leaving his arms empty and his pants too tight. "Tomorrow," she reminded him. "I'm picking the girls up from day camp."

"Right. The all-important costumes for the Medieval Faire."

"Yep. I'll have them home earlier this time."

"Stay for dinner? I'll have the food ready when you get here."

"Can't. I've got a hot date." She laughed, the sound musical. Teasing. "You should see your face."

"We have rules," he said darkly. "You. Me. No one else."

She bent down to him, nuzzled his cheek and

whispered, "It's so much fun to mess with you." Somehow, he kept from grabbing her and yanking her back down across his knees. She pulled away just enough to capture his gaze. "I'm meeting Erin and Carrie at Beach Street Brews."

Now he just wished he could go, too. Secret flings, he was quickly learning, had a whole raft of drawbacks.

His disappointment must have shown on his face, because she added, "They *are* my best friends. And I hardly see them these days, you know?"

"I get it." He needed to back off and he knew it. "Have a good time."

She put her mouth to his ear a second time. "I would rather be with you," she whispered. And then, with a quick brush of her cool lips to his cheek, she straightened and headed for the steps leading down off the deck. He watched her go until she disappeared into the shadows of the trees.

At a little past ten the next morning, Dante got a text from Connor Bravo—Lunch? Noon. Fisherman's Korner.

Alarm rattled through him. Suddenly he was certain Connor knew about him and Gracie. They would end up beating the crap out of each other the way they had a decade ago when Dante found out about Connor and Aly.

But then he reminded himself to get a damn grip. How would Connor know? Gracie wouldn't have said anything, and no one else knew. And besides, who even knew if it would bother Connor that Dante and Gracie were having a thing? Not all brothers went ballistic over stuff like that.

Still, it would be awkward, eating fish and chips with Connor, knowing that he'd been in Gracie's bed yesterday and couldn't wait to go there again.

Well, too bad, Dante decided. He and Gracie were nobody's business.

And he and Connor *were* friends—a hard-earned, lifelong friendship that had gone off the rails more than once, yet somehow always managed to end up back on track. A man needed to spend a little quality time with his friends.

Dante replied, I'll be there.

And it went pretty well. Connor was all about his baby daughter. They agreed that daughters made a man's life complete.

"Oh, and don't forget," Connor reminded him. "You're coming to the party next month, you and the girls."

On the fourth Saturday in July, at Oceanside Gardens, a fancy wooded estate and event venue just outside of town, Connor and Aly were celebrating their remarriage to each other. The original plan had been to have the party in October because they'd been married in October—both times. But Aly ended up deciding it would be more fun to have their reunion celebration in the summer. She wanted a sit-down dinner outside and dancing under the stars.

"We'll be there," promised Dante. Along with a whole bunch of friends and just about every Bravo and Santangelo in the USA.

"So how's it working out having Gracie living at the cabin?" Connor asked. Dante must have blinked or otherwise looked busted, because his best friend's forehead crinkled in confusion. "What?"

"Not a thing."

"You're acting weird, man."

Dante played it off with a shrug. "Gracie's great. My daughters and my dog are crazy about her." *And they are not alone.* "Owen spends half the damn time at the cabin with her. And she's got Harper fixing the girls up with costumes for the Medieval Faire. Nat and Nic are thrilled about that."

"I'm glad it's working out. Gracie really needed her own place."

"I'm glad to have her there." So glad. Connor

had no idea. Dante stared across the table at his friend and brother-in-law. For several years, he'd been certain he would never willingly speak to Connor again. And yet, here they were, sharing a booth at Fisherman's Korner, tight with each other just like it used to be. "Connor, I…" Where was he going? He wasn't quite sure. Somewhere he shouldn't, probably.

Connor ate his last steak fry. "Yeah?"

"I keep thinking about that fight we had."

"Which one?"

"When you and Aly first got together."

Connor arched an eyebrow and shook the ice in his nearly empty cup. "Yeah, that was a messy one."

"I was a complete jerk to have come after you like that. I acted like I owned you *and* my sister, like the two of you had no right to be together."

Connor set down the cup, his blue gaze assessing. "What's going on with you?"

Gracie. For as long as she'll put up with me. "I've been thinking that I never apologized to you for being such an ass."

"And this is it, then? Your apology?"

"Yeah. I'm sorry, Connor. I was wrong. You and Aly are good together. More than good. I think it was always supposed to be you and her. I'm glad that you worked it out and got back together. And I'm pissed at myself that I ever tried to stand in the way of what you guys have."

Connor's expression was completely unreadable—for about ten seconds. But then he nodded. "It's okay," he said gruffly.

"Is it?"

"Hell, yeah. You were out of line there at the first. But I was no hero when she and I broke up. You had a right to hate my dumb ass over that. It's just what it is. Crap happens. Everybody messes up. If you're lucky and you keep trying, you work it out somehow. We got through it. Over time. Me and Aly—*and* you and me."

Dante had to swallow the giant lump in his throat. "Yeah. I guess we did."

Connor reached across the table between them and clapped a hand on Dante's shoulder. "You're too hard on yourself."

"I don't think so. Not really."

"Yeah. Really. You and me, we're solid. Don't let what's over and done with eat you up, okay? Apology accepted."

"Gracie! Drink up." Carrie picked up Grace's beer and held it out to her.

"I am." Grace took the heavy glass mug and

set it down without taking a sip. It was her damn beer and she intended to drink it at her own pace—which was snail-like compared to Carrie and Erin. They'd gotten to the brew pub early and polished off a pitcher before she arrived.

Erin scoffed. "You are not keepin' up, girl-friend."

"You're not a schoolteacher yet," razzed Carrie.

Grace reminded herself that the two were half-sloshed and there was no point in taking anything they said too seriously. "Okay, you guys. I love you with all the love in the universe and beyond. But stop trying to pour beer down my throat. I can do that myself."

"You're no fun," whined Carrie.

"Yeah." Erin piled on. "It's like you don' really like us anymore."

"Not true." She had Carrie on one side and Erin on the other, so she wrapped an arm around each of them. "Love you both. Mean that."

They leaned their heads on her shoulders. Erin said kind of mournfully, "Love you, too…"

It was sad, really, when a girl and her two forever BFFs just weren't getting along.

The waitress appeared and set another pitcher on the table. "From the three hotties at the end of the bar." She tipped her head toward a trio of twentysomething guys who looked like maybe they worked in construction. They were all in worn jeans, heavy work boots and dark T-shirts, all three of them smirking, raising their beer mugs in unison.

Of course, Carrie signaled them over.

They started out on one side of the round table, with Grace and her friends on the other. Names were exchanged. Turned out one of the guys had graduated from Valentine Bay High the year Grace and her friends were freshman. One was from Astoria and the other had recently moved north from Coos Bay.

Took them about half an hour to start coupling up. The guy from Astoria, whose name was Keith, ended up focusing on Gracie. She nursed her second beer as he talked about high school, the construction company he worked for and his favorite band. It was all just a dance, everyone hooking up old-school, in a bar with alcohol, instead of on the apps. She wondered what she was doing here.

She could've had dinner with Dante and the girls.

Both Erin and Carrie got out their phones and snapped a bunch of pictures to post on Snapchat and Instagram. At seven thirty, Grace had had enough. She hooked her bag over her shoulder.

"Whoa," said Keith. "You're not leaving already?"

"Gracie, hold on." Carrie stopped whispering with the guy from Coos Bay and chimed in. "You can't go yet. It's early."

Grace dropped some bills on the table. "No, really. Gotta go."

"At least give me your number," Keith insisted.

"Sorry." She went ahead and just hit him with the truth. "I'm seeing someone."

"What?" Erin's mouth dropped open. "Who? Since when? There's a guy?"

"You never mentioned a guy," scoffed Carrie. She waved a hand. "You're lyin'."

"Yeah." Erin leaned on the local guy, who had his arm wrapped around her. "I don't know what's the matter with you lately, but you need to get over yourself."

For a moment, Grace just stood there, looking down at her best friends since childhood and three guys she didn't know. She had no idea what to say. She needed to sit down with her girls and talk about how lately they seemed to have nothing in common and she really didn't know what to do about that. Would a long talk solve anything—or just make the problem worse?

Who knew? And in any case, that talk wasn't

happening here at Beach Street Brews, with three strangers to witness it, the music too loud and everybody drinking. Nothing good was going to come from trying to face hard truths tonight.

Feeling like a stranger in her own life, she said, "I'll call you." With a quick nod to Carrie and then Erin, she turned and got out of there before someone said something they couldn't take back.

Dante heard Grace's RAV4 pull in at a little before eight. He made himself wait until Nic and Nat were settled in their room for the night before he sent Grace a text.

Meet you on the deck for a beer?

She answered right away, which eased all the annoying, formless fears that were chewing at the edges of his mind—completely unacceptable fears. That she would meet someone else and tell him it was over. That a night out with her girlfriends might remind her of all the ways she could be having a good time if only she hadn't agreed to be secretly exclusive with a divorced single dad.

They were having a fling. He shouldn't be taking this so damn seriously.

Too bad he didn't know any other way to be.

No beer for me, she wrote, but I'm on my way.

He resisted the burning need to shoot back, You drunk already? Because yeah, he was a jealous, controlling ass and he needed to make an effort not to show it.

A moment after he sat down at the outside table, she materialized out of the shadows. The moon made a silver halo around her pale hair. She wore a filmy top that slid off one shoulder and white shorts that clung to the perfect curves of her hips. Her smooth legs went on forever.

He rose as she came up onto the deck—that made it easier to reach for her when she got close enough to touch.

"Missed you." He kissed her. She tasted like all the best things, everything he wanted. He needed to try to remember that he didn't own her and what they had wasn't meant to last. It could never work out long-term with her for all kinds of reasons that right now seemed hazy and pretty much meaningless.

She sighed into his mouth and pulled away too soon.

"Come back here." He tried to claim her lips again.

But she put her palms against his chest, exerting a gentle but firm pressure. "If you want to keep this thing we have a secret, we can't be climbing all over each other when Natalie and Nicole are at home."

She was, unfortunately, right. If either of the girls got up and came out to the living area, they would have a clear view of whatever was happening out on the deck.

Reluctantly, he dropped back into his chair and picked up his beer.

She sat down across from him and smiled at the tall glass he'd brought out for her. "Ice water. Sometimes it's like you can read my mind." She picked it up and drank. He watched her pale, smooth throat move as she swallowed. She met his gaze when she set the glass down. "Where's Owen?"

"In with the girls." He asked, "So, good time with Erin and Carrie?"

"Not really."

He felt much too pleased to hear that. "What happened?"

"We're just not singing from the same playbook anymore. They were pushing drinks I didn't want at me and then when I got up to leave, they were pissed, said I was cutting out on them—oh, and don't believe anything you see on Snapchat or Instagram."

Wariness crawled up his spine. "Who took pictures of what?"

"These three guys bought us a pitcher. One of them ended up sitting next to me. Carrie and Erin whipped out their phones and started snapping away."

"This guy got a name?"

"Keith."

"Last name?"

"He never said." She gave him a long, steady look across the table. "He never even got that close. But social media is a swamp and you've got a jealous streak. I kind of figure full disclosure up front is the way to go with you."

He didn't even try to hide his slow smile. "How'd you get so smart about men?"

"Lots of annoying brothers and three summers in Europe."

He wanted to touch her again, to kiss her. To keep going from there. But that wasn't happening tonight. And he had a feeling she needed to talk more about her girlfriends. "So then, about Carrie and Erin…?"

Her beautiful mouth twisted down at the corners. "From their point of view, well, I used to be fun and now I'm a drag who thinks she's too good for them. We probably need a heart-to-heart, the three of us, but I'm kind of afraid that will only make the problem worse." She grinned across the table at him. "Aren't you sorry you asked?"

"Nope—and longtime friends go through changes. You can't always be on the same page. Give it time. The problem may work itself out on its own eventually."

She rubbed at the condensation on the side of her glass, her soft mouth drawn down in a thoughtful little frown. "Like you and Connor?"

"Yeah—and I had lunch with Conn today, as a matter of fact. It's all good with him and me now." *And as long as he doesn't find out about us, it's likely to remain that way.*

Gracie sat back in her chair. Gathering her hair in one hand, she slid a hair elastic off her wrist and anchored the thick, silky mass into a high ponytail. "Sometimes I see right through you, Officer. You're afraid he might find out about us and hit the roof over it. What you're forgetting is that Connor is not you and about a hundred years have passed since you two got into it because he had the balls to fall in love with Aly. Maybe he's learned something from what happened back then."

"Unlike me?"

"I didn't say you hadn't learned anything."

"Gracie. You think I'm a dinosaur."

Her ponytail bounced as she turned to face him

directly. "Don't put words in my mouth. You're definitely Homo sapiens. Or close. Neanderthal, maybe?"

Something like tenderness washed through him. She was not only gorgeous and funny and smart, she was strong. If she didn't like something he was doing, she said so. She had no qualms about giving him a bad time. Marj had been…softer, somehow. Less outgoing, less sure of herself. When they first met, at Portland State, he'd liked that she tended to defer to him, that she never really knew how to hold the line against him. He pushed. Marj gave way. It took her a year after their divorce to finally stand up to him and announce she was going to see other guys.

Gracie frowned across the table at him. "You're too quiet. What's going on?"

"I got a call from Marj today."

She watched him so closely, like she was picking up clues from his expression and body language. Gracie really cared how he was doing, what might be bothering him. "Everything okay?"

"Everything's fine. Marj always loved the Fourth of July in Valentine Bay. The parade in the Historic District, fireworks on the beach at night…"

"Wait. Your ex called to say she wants to come to town for the Fourth?"

"Yeah. And it was two calls. First, she called to feel me out about it. I said sure. She made a hotel reservation and then she called back to say that she and Roger would arrive in the afternoon on the third and go home the morning of the fifth. I invited them here for dinner on the third. She asked if they could join me and the girls for the fireworks and I said yes."

"That was nice of you."

"I'm not nice. We both know it. What else could I say but come on up and watch the fireworks with us? Marjorie is a good person and Roger is… Well, the girls really like him. Why shouldn't my ex and her new husband come into town for the holiday and watch the fireworks with Nic and Nat?"

Gracie reached across and put her hand over his. Her touch soothed and burned simultaneously. Was he in too deep with her, already? It sure felt like it. "You *are* nice, Dante. At least, on occasion. You really hate that your ex and her husband are coming, don't you?"

He wanted to drag her hand to his mouth and bite the back of it. "I don't hate it, no."

"You just *hate* it." Her white teeth flashed in a devilish smile.

"Exactly."

"It will be good, you'll see."

"I'll reserve judgment till after the fact."

She gave his hand a last, reassuring pat and pulled hers away. Somehow, he managed not to grab it back.

For a few minutes, neither of them said a word. They sipped their drinks and stared out at the night. It was a comfortable silence, the kind that happens between friends.

And they *were* friends. They had *been* friends before the night they ended up in his bed together.

The question was, would they still be friends when this crazy, hot thing between them burned itself out?

Thursday, Grace was at home in the cabin when Dante called at twenty minutes to noon.

She saw it was him and answered with one word. "Yes."

"Fifteen minutes." His voice, low and rumbly, caused every nerve in her body to snap to excited attention.

"I'll be naked."

And she was. Their second nooner was even better than the first.

Friday, Gracie picked up the girls from day

camp again. They stopped at the beach cottage on the way home for the finished Medieval Faire gowns.

Saturday, the Faire opened. Gracie wouldn't be going. She had to open at the Sea Breeze.

But early that morning she went to Dante's house for breakfast with him and the girls. Dante made them all waffles and eggs and then Gracie took Nic and Nat back to the cabin. She braided their long brown hair—French fishtail braids, woven with shiny ribbon to match the gowns that Harper had made. Since it was a costume event, Dante had grudgingly given permission for the girls to wear light makeup.

Grace supervised the application of cheek and lip color and mascara, too. They put on the gowns and the soft Mary Jane–style shoes Harper had found for them on Etsy.

"Gorgeous. Both of you," Gracie said, when they all three piled into the tiny bathroom so the girls could admire themselves in the full-length mirror that hung on the back of the door.

"Wow! These dresses turned out so good," said Natalie, her pretty face aglow. "Better even than I was hoping for."

Nicole, wide-eyed, nodded in agreement. "The braids are so beautiful."

"*You* are absolutely beautiful—both of you," Gracie said. Because they were.

She took them back out to the main room and gave her phone a workout, snapping pictures from just about every angle as they happily posed and preened.

They were the best, Nic and Nat. They brought it sharply home to Grace why people wanted kids. She could actually start to see herself with a husband and children—not now, of course. And no, not with Dante. He'd made it way clear it wasn't going to be him.

But the right guy. In time.

"Let's go show Daddy!" cried Nicole.

"Right now!" agreed Nat.

They trooped back to the main house, where Dante called them both beautiful. His voice was kind of gravelly, the way it got when something moved him. To Grace, he had that look—the look of a loving dad confronting the reality of how fast his daughters were growing up.

She took more pictures, some with her phone and some with Dante's. This time she had the girls pose on either side of their dad. All three of them were beaming, the girls out of pure happiness, Dante with such pride.

Then Natalie insisted, "Gracie, we need you in a picture, too."

"Yes!" agreed Nicole. "We need pictures with you."

Grace handed Dante back his phone and hers, too, and he did the honors.

After that, she got lots of hugs and thank-yous from both girls. She felt kind of sad to leave them, but she waved goodbye and returned to the cabin to get ready for work.

It was a gorgeous day, cool and clear with only a slight breeze. At the bar, Grace rolled up the wide garage-style door that led out to a big patio with a view of the beach and the endless blue ocean. She and Marianna, the waitress, set up the café tables and opened the umbrellas to shade them from afternoon sun.

They opened at eleven. By noon, they were packed. The Sea Breeze had a small kitchen in back. They served bar food—sliders and nachos, potato skins and hot wings. Grace called Ingrid at 12:30 and she came in at a little after 1:00 to help out. For the next three hours, Grace worked behind the bar, setting up, mixing and pouring nonstop.

When the crowd finally thinned out and she got a break, it was past four. She claimed her usual spot at the quiet end of the bar and Ingrid served her a tonic with lime and a nice big plate of nachos.

"You sharing?" asked a familiar deep voice behind her.

A thrill zinged her through her, just at the sound of his voice. She had it bad for him, no doubt about it. "Maybe."

Dante took the stool next to her and signaled Ingrid, who brought him a clean plate and his favorite pale ale. "I was kind of hoping I might catch you in a quiet moment."

"And you did." She was so glad to see him. It made the sweetest ache under her breastbone, to have him right there beside her. You'd think it had been months instead of a few hours since she'd left him and the girls that morning. He wore the same light blue T-shirt he'd had on then. The shirt showcased his big arms and ripped chest.

And she needed to quit staring at him like she'd rather have him than her nachos. She took a long sip of tonic. "What did you do with my two favorite medieval princesses?"

"One of the day camp moms took them to her house with her daughter and my niece and a couple of other girls. I got a call from my sister-in-law just before we left for the Faire, inviting them. There's a pool, evidently. They took their swimsuits and a change of clothes when we left the house. They're having a swim party and then hot dogs for dinner. I'll pick them up at eight."

And that meant he had three hours or so to himself.

Too bad she had to work until seven. "So, how was the Faire?"

"Packed with people."

"Excellent. A big success, then?"

He ate a chip, nodding. "Nat and Nic loved every minute of it. They were in the minstrel show and they demonstrated medieval dances they'd learned in day camp."

"I wish I could have been there."

"I've got pictures." He beamed a proud-father smile.

"Show me."

He got out his phone and handed it over. As she scrolled through the shots of his beautiful daughters at the Medieval Faire, he leaned close. "Come home with me."

She wanted to. So bad. "Can't. Gotta work."

"Secret flings are a pain in my ass," he muttered.

So let's just go public, she longed to suggest.

But she only went on looking at the pictures

and munching her nachos. She already wanted so much more from him than he was willing to give.

And she was far from ready to chance losing what she had of him on the off chance he might suddenly be willing to give her more.

Chapter Eight

The next day, Sunday, Dante took Nat and Nic to his parents' house for Sunday dinner. All four of his brothers were there. Pascal and Tony brought the wives and kids. Marco, at twenty, was still single. And Mac, the baby, had turned nine months old the week before. Aly, Connor and baby Emelia had gone to Daniel Bravo's this Sunday. Gracie had said she would be at Daniel's, too.

Dante sat at his mom's long dining room table and ate her amazing pot roast and fantasized about what it might be like if he had Gracie beside him. It was only a dream. He knew it. And he'd never been much for dreamy imaginings.

But lately, well, sometimes he couldn't help himself. And being dreamy about Gracie felt damn good.

He wore a smile on his face a lot more than usual lately. No, he didn't get enough time with her. But when he did, he made every minute count. And when he had to leave her, he had the next time with her to look forward to. Even when he couldn't be alone with her, he saw her coming and going along the graveled road that ran by the house, saw the lights on in the cabin and knew she was in there. At least a couple of times a week, he lured her onto his deck after dark so they could hang out together for an hour or so, talking about whatever they had on their minds while simultaneously trying to keep their hands off each other.

His brother Pascal elbowed him in the ribs and muttered out of the side of his mouth, "Mom's talking to you."

He turned his head to meet his mother's blue eyes. "What, Mom?"

"I said, you look like a man in love." Catriona O'Leary Santangelo beamed him a wide, beautiful smile. "It's a good look on you, Dante."

"No clue what you're talking about." His mother was too damn perceptive by half—not that he was in love with Gracie. He was just...

Okay, he wasn't sure what to call it. Crazy. Wild. Out of his mind for her. All those things. It was called chemistry and it felt like nothing else because the chemistry with Gracie?

Off the freaking charts. Like no chemistry he'd ever experienced before. It helped him to understand the power of the attraction between Aly and Connor—and his own mom and dad.

But, as he continually reminded himself, for him and Gracie, it wasn't the kind of thing that was meant to last. She was young with a lot to do in her life, and he was divorced and set in his ways. It was only for right now and it was amazing. And somehow, when it was over, he would find a way to keep his friendship with her.

"What's her name?" asked his mother as she picked a slice of cooked carrot out of Mac's hair and set it back on his high chair tray.

"Oooo-bah!" crowed Mac. He grabbed the bit of carrot and shoved it in his face.

And Dante's mom was still looking right at him, waiting for an answer. The whole table was a little too quiet, he thought.

His dad came to his rescue. "Leave the man alone, Cat," said Ernesto with a chuckle. "Whatever he's dreamin' about, he's not sharing it at the dinner table."

* * *

Both Tuesday and Wednesday of the following week, he joined Gracie in the cabin in the early afternoon. With Gracie, each time was better than the last.

Life was good. So good that he was much more patient when his daughters compared him negatively to the wonderful, perceptive, thoughtful, permissive Roger.

So good that when Marjorie and Roger arrived on the third of July, he happily grilled them all burgers out on the deck and felt only minimal resentment toward the stepfather his girls adored. Gracie had to work that night. She left the cabin at around five thirty, shortly after Roger and Marj arrived. They were all out on the deck and he was firing up the grill when her RAV4 emerged from the trees.

"Grace!" Marj called. She said to Roger. "I haven't seen her in years." She got up and ran down the side steps to intercept the RAV4. Marj leaned in Gracie's window. He could hear their voices faintly, though not the words they exchanged. The sound of Gracie's laughter floated on the breeze, causing a tightness under Dante's breastbone, a rising feeling full of heat and tenderness. He wished she could blow off the Sea Breeze for the night, come have burgers on the deck with him and the family.

And there was nothing out of line about wishing that. Because they were not only lovers on the down-low, they were friends.

Roger, at the table, asked, "So, new tenant?"

"Gracie? Yeah, she's using the cabin for as long as she needs it." It just felt weird, to talk about Gracie with Roger—but then, talking about anything with Roger always felt weird to him. "She's a good friend." *And so much more.* Not that Roger was ever going to know that.

Nic, who knelt on the deck boards brushing Owen with her Princess Jasmine hairbrush, started in about the Medieval Faire and the costumes Gracie had arranged for her sister to make for them.

Nat, at the table next to Roger, chimed in with praise for Gracie—and her sisters, Harper and Hailey, too.

Over in the driveway, Marj stepped back from Gracie's car. She waved and Gracie drove away. Dante felt bereft.

Was he ridiculous?

No doubt about it.

"You seem a little…pensive." Roger was still looking at him.

Marj chuckled as she dropped into the chair on

Roger's other side. "Darling, don't analyze my ex." It was a command. Marj was so perky and bossy with Roger, like a whole different woman from the one Dante had once been married to. It was kind of disorienting. He felt glad she was happy, but found it strange to see this other, more assertive side of her, nonetheless.

"Sorry, my love." Roger leaned in. They shared a quick kiss, after which Nic and Nat dragged them both into the house. A moment later, he heard Nat singing "Let It Go" at the top of her lungs.

Owen, stretched out on the deck not far from the table, lifted his head and let out a howl, just singing along.

The next day, the Fourth, Dante and the girls met Marj and Roger for a late breakfast at the Tufted Puffin Café down in the Valentine Bay Historic District. They wandered around window-shopping for a while and then watched the parade, which consisted of floats created by local organizations and businesses and various service vehicles. Once that was over, Marj and Roger went off on their own. Dante took Nic and Nat to his brother Tony's for a family barbecue.

At nine thirty that night, they arrived at Valentine Beach, where they met up with Marj and

Roger and just about everybody else in town. Dante brought a couple of blankets and his ancient boom box.

Launched from a barge offshore, the fireworks started at ten. The local radio station played music synchronized to the display. Dante turned his boom box to the right station, as did at least a hundred others up and down the beach. It was quite the extravaganza.

His daughters sat on either side of him, staring up at the night sky, transfixed. Marj leaned her head on Roger's shoulder. Kind of a perfect end to another Independence Day.

Except…

Dante's mind wouldn't stop straying to thoughts of Gracie. She had the closing shift again at the Sea Breeze. He wanted to get out his phone and send her some silly text, just to let her know he was thinking of her.

But she was working and probably wouldn't check her phone for hours yet anyway. And the girls and Marj and Roger were bound to notice if he got on his phone in the middle of the fireworks.

They weren't a couple, him and Gracie. He needed to keep that thought firmly in mind. If she was here with them right now, he would have to play it strictly friends only, because those were the rules he himself had laid down. He wouldn't even be able to put his arm around her, let alone steal a kiss as "Born in the USA" filled the air and bottle rockets exploded overhead.

And come on, even if she'd had the day off, she very well might have planned to meet up with her sisters and brothers or a couple of girlfriends. He had no real claim on her and he needed to remember that. It was only for now and that was how they both wanted it.

"Hey, guys…" As if he'd conjured her straight from his own out-of-control fantasies, there she was, wearing a Sea Breeze T-shirt, white Chucks and white jeans, that sleek waterfall of platinum hair in a high ponytail. She grinned down at them.

"Gracie!" his daughters cried in gleeful unison.

"Happy Independence Day." Marj beamed up at her, and Roger gave her a friendly nod of greeting.

"Sit with us," demanded Nat.

As a sparkly globe of purple light burst open in the night sky and Katy Perry's voice blared from the speakers up and down the beach, Nicole jumped up, grabbed Gracie's hand and pulled her down to the blanket. "Isn't it beautiful?" Nicole leaned into her.

Gracie fondly nudged Nic's shoulder with her own. "Spectacular."

It just so happened that Dante was on Gracie's other side. He almost didn't dare to look at her for fear that all his aching, confused emotions would show on his face.

Really, it wasn't supposed to be like this, not for him. He understood himself, knew too well his own hotheaded nature and had spent most of his adult life trying to keep a lid on it. Injustice and insults, bad stuff some people did to others— all that got to him more than it did to the average guy. He was one of those men who could fly off the handle, go off like a human bottle rocket if he didn't make an effort to keep his emotions under strict control. He'd learned to carefully consider just about every move he made. He tried to do the right thing, take good care of his girls and just generally lead a useful, productive life.

And until that fateful night a month ago when he'd invited Gracie over to cry on his shoulder, he thought he'd been doing a pretty good job of all that.

But now...

Well, how did she do it—give him all these damn *feelings*? He'd never trusted feelings. Too often, they made people do stupid things.

And he was being doubly ridiculous now, acting like a twelve-year-old with his first crush. He'd wanted her here with the burning fire of a thousand suns. And yet somehow, now that she was sitting right next to him, he'd yet to so much as say hi to her, let alone glance over and meet her eyes.

Carefully, he turned his head.

She was looking right at him, a slow, devilish grin curving those perfect, shell-pink lips. He got a whiff of her perfume, equal parts sweet and tart. It sent a spike of heat straight to his groin. He drew his legs up and wrapped his arms around his knees to disguise his response to the barest hint of her scent.

"Back at the Sea Breeze, everyone's out on the patio watching the fireworks," she said. "Ingrid gave me an hour-long break."

"I'm glad," he heard himself say.

One sleek eyebrow lifted. "About what?"

Holding eye contact seemed dangerous. He glanced upward as bright balls of light with thick, glittery tails shot upward from the water, fanning out as they rose. The opening strains of "The Star-Spangled Banner" swelled on the cool evening wind.

She nudged him with an elbow.

He leaned into her and whispered, "I'm glad that you're here."

She laughed, the sound filling him with equal parts joy and pain. It was like nothing he'd ever known before, to feel the way she made him feel. He hated it.

But he kind of loved it, too.

The next week, Grace and Dante stole two long lunches together, on Tuesday and Thursday. Instead of food, they had each other. Both times were the best time ever—and each encounter was much too short. Too soon, she would find herself standing in the cabin doorway, wearing nothing but panties and a tank top or a wrinkled T-shirt, her tangled hair in her eyes, feeling all kinds of lazy and sexually satisfied as she waved him goodbye.

The weekend after the Fourth, a minor miracle occurred. The girls' day camp counsellors took Nic and Nat and several other local kids on a weekend campout over Friday and Saturday night. Gracie worked both nights, but Dante was on his summer schedule, which meant the weekends were his.

When she arrived at the cabin in the very early hours of Saturday morning, he was waiting on the front step with Owen. They spent the rest of the night together and all of the next day too, making love for hours, sharing every meal, taking Owen for long walks down on the beach. Saturday night at six, she left him reluctantly to go to work.

"Be in my bed when I get home," she commanded as she kissed him goodbye.

He lifted his mouth from hers just long enough to reply, "Count on it." And then he was kissing her again, deeply. At length.

She arrived home at a quarter to three Sunday morning to find him right where she'd told him to be. He held back the covers. She stripped off her clothes and joined him.

It was so good with Dante. She never wanted it to end.

And he seemed pretty taken with her, too. More than once that magical weekend, she seriously considered broaching the subject of where they might go from here, of actual dating, doing more than each other, like maybe dinner and a show. They could take it slow, go only places where they were unlikely to run into anyone they knew.

Time in bed with him was the absolute best. But she liked him so much—as a lover, as a friend, as someone really special to her in so many ways. She just couldn't stop wishing they could be together without sneaking around.

She kept trying to come up with the right words to broach the "next level" conversation. But she was nervous to approach him about it. He'd been so firm that he didn't want anyone else to know they had a thing together.

Why didn't he, really? The more she thought about this secret they were keeping, the more she wondered why they even needed it to be a secret.

She needed to ask him about that, talk it out with him. Too bad the right words never seemed to come to her.

And then all of a sudden, it was Sunday afternoon and he had to go pick up the girls at Valentine City Park.

The next week was not so great, secret fling–wise. When Dante could get away, she couldn't. And the other way around. Twice, they met on his back deck after his daughters were in bed. They would each have a beer. Mostly, what they talked about was how not getting together was driving them both a little bit crazy. Somehow, though, they managed to keep their hands off each other. If one of them would weaken, the other would mention that they were in full view of the living area should the twins decide to leave their room.

That Saturday, it was the girls' turn to host a sleepover. Nicole and Natalie invited their cousin Heather and three more of their Valentine Bay friends. Sunday, Dante took the girls to his parents' house for dinner and Grace went to Daniel's.

By Monday, she was feeling a little depressed at how difficult having a secret fling could be. Her schedule and Dante's just weren't matching up and that made her sad.

Was she getting too attached?

Well, the guy had made it painfully clear that what they had was *all* they would have. He'd given no indication he was ready to change things up, and she'd never quite figured out how to talk to him about that.

On the plus side, when they did manage to slip off alone, it was fabulous. Mostly, she really loved it, having it be just the two of them, just for now, nobody's business. The limited time they had together kept both of them focused on making every minute count.

Still, it was starting to get old. It was starting to remind her that she'd never really had a guy who was all hers, straight up, for everyone in town to see. Niall and Keegan and Paolo were across an ocean in another world and just for the summer.

Yeah, she'd had a couple of "serious" boyfriends in high school, but she was a kid then, with a very protective big brother. Daniel used to make her leave the bedroom door open whenever a boy came over. And when she finally did have sex her senior year, it was in Randy Daughtry's ancient Ford Courier pickup.

Ugh. In some ways, all this sneaking around

with Dante made her feel like a teenager again. And just lately, not in a good way.

She needed someone to talk to about it. A little quality time with her BFFs would really help. She texted Carrie. When she didn't hear back in the next few hours, she tried Erin.

Erin's reply was not encouraging. What? U got a minute to spare 4 us now?

Well, that just made her feel worse than ever. Hurt and sad and more than a little bit angry, she stared at Erin's text and had no idea what her reply ought to be.

They needed to talk. And probably not about Dante. First and foremost, they had to deal with what had gone wrong in their friendship, the friendship that they'd always vowed would last their whole lives. Grace really didn't know what she'd done to piss them off. It was time she found out. Can we talk?

Erin wrote back, Bout what?

Are you at home? I'll come over.

Whatevs

Grace decided to consider that a yes. I'm on my way.

At the two-bedroom apartment in a ten-unit

complex on Pine Avenue, she found both Carrie and Erin at home.

Erin let her in with a sigh and a heavily ironic, "Well, look who finally showed up."

Carrie sat on the sofa drinking a canned Bloody Mary, an open pizza box on the coffee table in front of her. She raised the can. "Been a while."

"Drink?" asked Erin with zero enthusiasm.

Grace figured maybe attempting to be social would pave the way for her a little, get them off to a decent start. "Sure, thanks."

Carrie swept out a hand toward the fridge. "Help yourself." Erin plunked down beside her on the sofa.

Grace got a hard lemonade and took the chair across the coffee table from them. There was a moment. Dead silence. They stared at her and she returned the favor.

Finally, Grace waded in. "So lately, it's seemed like we're kind of drifting apart, you know?" Okay, yeah. Weak. But she had to start somewhere.

"You're always busy," Erin accused.

"Too busy for us, anyway," Carrie threw in with a toss of her head.

"You never want to chillax," said Erin. "You've always gotta be somewhere. It's no fun and it's like we don't even know you."

"And what about Keith?" demanded Carrie. It took Grace a moment to remember the guy at Beach Street Brews. And Carrie knew it, too. She scoffed. "You don't even remember Keith."

"No, I do." Grace knew she sounded superdefensive. She had no reason to be defensive. But somehow, she felt that way. "Of course, I remember Keith."

"He's a good guy and he really liked you and you just…" Shaking her head, Erin blew a raspberry.

Carrie waved her Bloody Mary. "All of a sudden, you're seeing someone—someone you so far haven't bothered to mention to your two best friends for just about your whole life?"

Grace realized that, at this point, there was no way she was talking to her supposed BFFs about Dante. Just wasn't going to happen. "Listen, who I'm seeing and whether or not I wanted to give Keith my number? Come on, you guys. This isn't about men. This is about you and me and why you're so angry at me lately."

"We told you." Erin took a long drink of her canned margarita. "You're always busy. You never want to hang with us…"

Carrie said, "It's like we don't really have much in common anymore."

Was it like that?

Yeah.

Grace sat a little straighter. "Well, so what?"

Carrie blinked at her and Erin gasped.

Grace leaned in across the coffee table. "Look. Maybe in life people don't always see things the same way. Maybe I'm all absorbed right now in stuff that bores you guys silly. So what? I love you both and I always will. You matter to me. A lot. And I really hope I still matter to you."

Another long silence crawled by.

And then Carrie said softly, "Oh," and burst into tears. Erin started crying, too. Grace felt the moisture welling in her own eyes.

They all three jumped up at the same time. Carrie and Erin darted around the coffee table for a group hug.

"Okay," Erin sniffled. "Maybe we were kind of being bitches about this."

"But we *miss* you," cried Carrie. "We need to see you more."

"You're right." Grace took the tissue Erin offered her and dabbed at her eyes. "Once every week or two, at least, we need to get together, no matter what."

And then Erin, looking thoughtful, qualified, "But then, we gotta accept that maybe sometimes that won't happen and just make it work when we can."

"And not get all judgy," Carrie added. Looking sweetly remorseful, she blew her nose.

They sat down again. Grace finished her drink and said yes to a second one and a slice of cold pizza. Carrie and Erin filled her in on what she'd been missing.

Both of her friends were still working at the same upscale restaurant in Astoria. Carrie had said yes to a second date with the guy from Coos Bay. Erin was still keeping things strictly casual on the relationship front.

Grace explained that yeah, she was seeing someone exclusively. But he wanted to keep it just between the two of them, so she was respecting his privacy.

"A secret love is kind of romantic," offered Erin in a hopeful tone.

"And fun?" Carrie put a question mark on the end of that.

Grace laughed. "Meaning, am I having a good time with him? Yeah. Super good."

Her friends said that was all that mattered and she left it at that. They set a date to get together next Monday, when all three of them were off work. Erin and Carrie would come to the cabin for dinner.

"About time we saw your new place," grumbled

Erin. And then she laughed. "Not that we're bitter or anything."

"Yeah," agreed Carrie. "Sometimes we're bitches, but we love you so much!"

There was more hugging. "Next Monday. My place. Six o'clock," Grace reminded them as she went out the door.

She got in behind the wheel of her car and paused to check her phone. There was a text from Dante. He'd sent it while she was with her friends.

God, I miss you. Come over for dinner with me and the girls? Another text came through as she was starting to reply. He wrote, So much for dinner, then. Meet me on the deck, 9:15?

She answered smiling, feeling eager and happy, just to know she would see him soon. I'll be there. Sorry about dinner. I've been at Carrie and Erin's. Just coming home now.

Be naked, he suggested—well, it was more of a command.

She laughed out loud. I'm thinking maybe we shouldn't risk scarring your daughters for life.

The sacrifices a man makes for his children, he replied.

The night was overcast, but Grace could see Dante clearly—the outline of his broad shoulders, the shine to his thick, dark hair. He was waiting for her at the table on the deck, limned by the spill of golden light from the fixture by the slider. No sign of Owen. He must be in with the girls.

Dante stood as she approached. "We haven't been alone in over a week." He was scowling.

"Wait. Is that an accusation?"

"It's a fact and I hate it." He grabbed her hand. "Come here." His warm touch sent a thrill of longing sizzling through her.

"The windows," she reminded him.

"This way." He pulled her across the deck and down the steps on the far side.

"Um, where are we going?" she asked as she trotted along behind him.

"Right here." He ducked under the canopy of a big leaf maple a few yards from the side of the house. "Nice and dark. No one will see us. And we'll hear if the girls come looking for me." He reeled her in close and put those big arms around her.

She whispered his name in eager welcome as his mouth came down on hers.

Wrapped up in Dante's arms, protected in tree shadow, Grace surrendered to the man she couldn't get enough of, to his body pressing so close to hers, to the hungry perfection of his kiss. Now and then he would lift his head—but only to slant his mouth the other way and claim her lips again.

"We're like a couple of hormonal kids," she remarked breathlessly.

"Just kiss me." And he took her mouth once more.

She felt better about this secret fling of theirs now that he was holding her, surer that this thing between them was the *right* thing. Yeah, she wanted more. But what they had in this moment was pretty darn spectacular.

And it didn't end with kissing. Eventually, his hand glided between their bodies and eased her zipper down. And then his fingers were there, working their magic.

He swallowed her moans as she went over the edge.

She returned the favor, going to her knees on the soft, mossy ground, taking charge of him in the most elemental way, reaching one hand up over his hard belly and ripped chest to cover his mouth and muffle his groans when he came.

"Come up here," he whispered roughly, taking her by the shoulders, pulling her upward until she was back in the cradle of his strong arms.

For several sweet minutes, they held each other. She tucked her head against his throat and he stroked her hair.

Then, when they were both breathing normally again, he knelt and brushed the damp moss off the knees of her jeans. Rising, cradling her face in his big hands, he kissed her once more, this time gently, with melting tenderness.

Then he led her back to the deck, where they sat together under the stars.

Again, she considered broaching the subject of changing things up a little between them, taking a step or two toward going public as a couple.

But before she could frame the words, he mentioned Nicole and Natalie. "Twelve more days and they're on their way back to Portland," he said.

"It's hard, huh, to let them go?"

"Yeah. I love it when they get here, hate it when they leave. The house always seems too big and way too quiet."

She reached across the table and took his hand in reassurance. "You're doing a great job with them—both you and Marjorie, I think. They're happy and outgoing and they have a lot of friends."

He wove his fingers with hers, but only for a moment before pulling away.

It wasn't fair that she felt hurt. They did have an agreement. But it caused an ache deep inside her, that they couldn't even hold hands for fear Nic and Nat might see and get the wrong idea.

Which really *wasn't* the wrong idea at all.

"It's after ten," she said, and stood. "I should go."

"Wait. What? You can't stay a few minutes longer?"

"No. I need to get back. I've got the day shift tomorrow."

"You go in at what, eleven?"

"Ten thirty. And I was hoping to get an hour or two before that to work on my lesson plans for the coming year." It was true, as far as it went. Her first year of teaching would be extrachallenging. She had to build her class curriculum from scratch. And she wouldn't be able to get into her classroom until right before school started. The more she had done before the mad scramble at the beginning of the term, the better.

He stared up at her, his face shadowed with the light behind him. "What'd I do?"

"Not a thing." It wasn't a lie, exactly. It was just, well, they were going nowhere and she was growing tired of standing still.

Tonight didn't feel like the right time to get into it, though. She didn't want to lose him—well, as much as she had of him.

But then, after the girls left for Portland at the end of the month, they would have more time alone together. That might be the best course for her, to wait until his daughters were with their mother and then bring up the possibility of her and Dante becoming…more to each other.

He stood. "You need to tell me what I did, so I can grovel and make it better."

She laughed. "You're not allowed to grovel on the back deck—not as long as the girls are here. They might see and then you'd have some serious explaining to do."

"You're right. Damn it." He started to reach for her—and stopped himself. His hand dropped to his side. "You're sure you're okay?"

She gave him a slow smile. "I am amazing."

"Oh, yes you are."

"Good night, Dante."

"'Night."

She turned and got out of there before she caved and hung around for another hour, longing to be closer to him, not daring to so much as reach for his hand.

Chapter Nine

That week turned out the same as the week before. Grace's schedule never meshed with Dante's.

Thursday, she went in to work at nine to help Ingrid with payroll, bills, ordering and miscellaneous other stuff. At six, she was finished for the night.

She started to head home, but then found herself turning left instead of right, headed for the cottage where Hailey and Harper lived. Both of their cars were parked in the wide space not far from the house. Grace pulled her RAV4 in beside them.

Hailey was standing in the open doorway to the screened porch, waiting for her as she came up the walk. "Want some dinner? It's Harper's awesome slow cooker burgundy beef tips with noodles. And I believe you've had my spinach strawberry salad before."

"With poppy seed dressing?" Grace asked hopefully.

"Of course."

"Yum. Suddenly, my stomach's growling."

Hailey wrapped her in a hug and then ushered her inside. "Right this way."

The food was ready, so they set another place for Grace. She poured three waters and Hailey poured the wine.

"I'm so glad I dropped by out of nowhere," Grace said. She ate another bite of beef and noodles. "Harper. This is so good."

Harper saluted with her wineglass.

They talked for a while about what was coming up for Harper and Hailey. They had their own little company, H&H Productions. Besides planning the occasional kids' party, they were working with the local arts council now, producing a series of seasonal community events—the Medieval Faire in the summer, a Fall Festival in October that culminated in a haunted house. Then over the holidays, they would put on the Christmas Extravaganza at the Valentine Bay Theater, an old movie theater down in the Historic District.

After the meal, they cleared off the table and cleaned up the kitchen together. The process kind of reminded her of the old days up at the house on Rhinehart Hill, all of them pitching in to get the household chores done.

They sat back down around the table. Harper poured them each another glass of wine.

"Okay." Hailey turned to Grace. "What's on your mind?"

Grace swirled the wine in her glass. "I'm that obvious?"

"Only to your wise and wonderful big sisters," replied Harper.

She grinned across the table at them, but the grin faded as she tried to figure out where to begin. "Well, there is something…"

"Tell all," commanded Hailey.

"It's, um, a secret thing. The deal is, I can't tell anyone."

"But you *have* to have someone to talk to," said Harper.

"And whatever you tell us," added Hailey, "we won't tell anyone else. Ever."

"Total cone of silence?" Gracie asked sheepishly.

"Total," agreed Hailey. She and Harper looked at each other, then back at Grace. The two nodded in unison. "We will tell no one," vowed Harper as Hailey nodded some more.

Grace squeezed her eyes shut and drew in a slow breath. "I'mhavingasecretflingwithDante Santangelo." The words came out in a rush as she exhaled.

Her sisters just stared.

Hailey spoke first, in an awed whisper. "Dante Santangelo. Really?"

"Yep."

Harper said, "He's so…serious."

"But hot," Hailey added.

Harper was nodding again. "Undeniably hot."

Hailey enjoyed a slow sip from her own glass. "I have to say, sexy action with a hot cop sounds like a pretty great thing to me."

Harper pushed her glass out of the way and stacked her forearms on the table. "Hasn't he been divorced forever?"

"Six years or so, yeah."

Grace's sisters shared yet another of those speaking glances and Grace felt that familiar stab of envy at their closeness. The two of them could have whole conversations just with their eyes, no actual words required.

Harper said, "Full disclosure, we did kind of wonder if there was something going on between you two when you moved into that cabin at his place, but then you did say he was just doing you a favor…"

"And he was. He *is*. He gave me the cottage for as long as I want it. Because he's a good guy and a good friend. As for our fling, we decided not to go public, to keep it just between us. Plus, well…"

"Say it," coaxed Hailey.

"He thinks he's too old for me and he has this thing about romantic love. Like he doesn't approve of it or he's just no good at it? I'm not sure exactly. His parents are happily married and so are two of his brothers. And Aly and Connor. He thinks he failed at love because it didn't work out with his ex-wife and now she's happily remarried—so it can't be *her* fault the marriage didn't work. It's like he blew it once and he won't try again."

"You think he's still in love with the ex?" asked Harper.

Did she think that? "No. No, I really don't. I think he's over Marjorie. She's a good person and they do a great job as coparents. They truly do."

Harper reached across and fondly brushed the back of Grace's hand. "For someone who's just having fun, you don't look all that happy—and if you're not happy, you should either move on or change the rules."

"Both options suck," Gracie said. "I do want more. But I don't want to lose what we have." Her sisters gazed at her with real sympathy. "And you know, I don't think changing the rules *is* an option, to be painfully honest about it. Dante was way clear that he's not up for anything more than what we have. He likes his life just the way it is. He told me he doesn't want a relationship and he's never getting married again."

Harper scoffed. "No offense, but Dante is being an idiot about this."

Gracie gave a sad little laugh. "Yeah, there's that."

Hailey said quietly, "You need to tell that man what *you* want."

"I'm afraid to," Grace admitted. "If I ask for more and he turns me down, what can I do but call it off? I mean, a girl needs to have *some* pride, right?"

"Yeah," said Hailey. "From that standpoint, you're kind of stuck."

"And if I call it off with him, it's going to hurt. Bad. And that's just more proof that I'm in deeper with him than I ever planned to get." Another forlorn chuckle escaped her. "I guess that makes me as much of an idiot as he is."

"You are *not* an idiot," Hailey said in a lecturing tone. And then she frowned. "Wait. You know what? Now and then, we're *all* idiots."

Harper suggested, "You could tell him what you *don't* want without making it an ultimatum. You could say that the way things are isn't working for you anymore. And then see where he takes it from there."

"But what if where he takes it is straight to goodbye? Uh-uh. I'm just not ready to chance that. It's not like he wasn't up front with me from the start. I believed him when he said he didn't want a real relationship..."

"You're totally gone on him, aren't you?" asked Harper gently.

"I am, yes. And the more I think it over, the more I realize that for right now, I'm still willing to go on as we have been. Rocking our fragile *non*relationship boat could be the end of what we do have. And just possibly the end of our friendship, too. I'm not ready to risk all that—not yet, anyway."

"The time is coming, though?" asked Hailey.

Grace hummed low in her throat, a sound of reluctant agreement. In response, Hailey got up and pulled her out of her chair and into a hug. Harper piled on. They stood there in the kitchen, the three of them, hugging it out.

Nothing had been resolved.

And yet, a half an hour later, when Grace climbed in her SUV, she felt better, just to have two smart, thoughtful women she trusted to talk it over with. She felt closer to her sisters than she ever had before.

Up till now, she'd kind of seen herself as a loose end among her siblings, the baby trailing after the bigger kids, a little bit left out, often left behind. To have Harper and Hailey rally around her, take her problems seriously and treat her like an equal?

It lifted her spirits and had her feeling a lot better about her place in the family.

Stolen moments with Gracie.

Dante didn't get enough of them. Friday at ten in the morning, he was just about to text her in hopes she might be home at lunchtime. But then he got a good lead on an ongoing case. He followed it and before he knew it, the day was mostly gone.

Friday night, his niece Heather slept over. He let the girls stay up late. When they finally settled down, it was almost eleven. He went outside to nurse a beer on the off chance the lights might be on at the cabin.

The porch light glowed at him through the trees, but that was it. Like a long-gone fool, with Owen at his heels, he jogged through the trees to get a closer look.

Nobody home, the windows all dark.

For a moment, he just stood there, wishing for things he was never going to have.

But then Owen whined and Dante shook himself. Not wanting to leave the girls alone for too long, he set off at a run for the main house. Dropping into a chair at the table, he took a long drink from his beer.

Owen plunked his head in Dante's lap. He gave the mutt a good scratch around the ears. "Our girl isn't home, buddy."

He got out his phone and started to text her. But then he dropped the phone on the table without finishing the text. No point. It was eleven at night and she was probably working.

And if she wasn't working, if she was out having a good time with her friends, he didn't even want to know.

What he wanted was more time with her.

And he would have it. Soon. A week from tomorrow, Nic and Nat went back to Portland. He would miss them a lot. But at least this year there was an upside to their going: more time with Gracie.

He couldn't wait for that.

And tomorrow was Aly and Connor's party at Oceanside Gardens. Gracie would be there, too. Maybe they could sneak away for a little while.

At the very least, he'd get a dance with her. Because even though this hot, perfect thing between them was a secret, why shouldn't he dance with his good friend Grace?

And why did it piss him off, that he had to make excuses for dancing with her?

Too much pissed him off lately. He wanted more of her, but he didn't want to think too hard about what that might mean.

The whole point was to have a good time, not take things too seriously, he kept reminding himself. When it ended, they would still be friends.

Not that he could imagine it ending anytime soon.

Aly and Connor's big party was an afternoon-to-evening event, with dinner and music and dancing. The weather was just about perfect, in the high seventies, a few wispy clouds drifting across the otherwise clear sky. Dante and his daughters arrived at a little after three.

Oceanside Gardens, a sprawling estate north of town surrounded by old-growth forest, lived up to its name. The garden paths seemed to go on forever, winding endlessly through thick plots of greenery and lush flowerbeds.

Aly had hired a six-piece band. Party lights were strung from every tree and post. The tables, set with fine china and white linen, were crowned with centerpieces of white pillar candles in big glass bowls of brilliant-colored dahlias.

For the kids, Aly and Connor had provided a giant ball pit shaped like a castle and filled with what looked like thousands of brightly colored balls. The pit had a slide you could ride down into the balls and a jungle gym suspended above them. Each child got a plastic jar of bubbles and a variety of wands of all sizes and shapes. Bubbles floated in the air all afternoon.

And if the little Santangelos and Bravos didn't want to blow bubbles or bounce around the ball pit, Aly had a face-painting station and a table full of art supplies set up in the garden's giant gazebo. The parents took turns supervising the fun.

Nicole and Natalie seemed to be having the best time of their lives. There was a lot of happy shouting and way too many gleeful, ear-piercing screams.

An hour or so before dinner, when Dante got a moment with his sister, he gave her the praise she deserved. "Killer party, Aly. You really out-did yourself."

She beamed him her beautiful smile. "I did, didn't I?"

"It's great. How's my baby niece?"

"She's good. Connor's got her somewhere around here…"

Aly and Connor pretty much had it all now. They were in love with each other and their baby daughter. They'd had a rough road, spent too many years apart. But in the end, here they were, sur-rounded by family, celebrating their second mar-riage to each other. They were happy and Dante was happy *for* them.

But that didn't mean he wouldn't razz his sister at least a little. "Too bad those dresses my girls are wearing will never be the same." The girls were rumpled and sweaty, their party dresses smeared with face paint and grass stains. Funny how Nic had a virtual meltdown when she accidentally spilled her soda in her lap at Camp 18—but when there was face painting and rolling on the grass in-volved, neither she nor her sister cared much what condition their clothes ended up in.

Aly just shrugged at his grumbling. "It's called having fun and your daughters are good at it."

"You always were a troublemaker," he grumbled some more, trying hard to look disapproving.

"Get over yourself," Aly dryly advised.

Right then, Nat shrieked with laughter as some redheaded kid Dante didn't recognize dragged her down off the jungle gym and into the ball pit. Dante shook his head. "I think I need a drink."

"Have a good time, big brother." Aly leaned in close and kissed his cheek, after which he headed for the open bar.

Dante got himself a beer and then, very casually of course, went looking for Gracie. He spotted her more than once. She wore a silky blue sundress that tied with little bows at the shoulders, her long white-gold hair like a waterfall down her back. She looked sweet and delicious and he wanted to eat her right up.

Not possible at this party, but hey, a guy could dream. He would settle for just standing close to her, breathing in the fresh, flowery scent of her skin, imagining all the things he would do to her as soon as he finally got her alone.

Unfortunately, every time he would try to work his way toward her, some relative or long-time friend would grab his arm and start talking his ear off about how his daughters were growing up so fast, and the summer had been so mild this year, hadn't it? And how were things with the Valentine Bay PD?

At dinner, Dante sat with Nicole, Natalie, his brother Pascal and Pascal's family. Percy and Daffodil Valentine claimed two other chairs at the table. Brother and sister and well into their eighties now, neither Percy nor Daffy had ever married. The last of the Valentines for which Valentine Bay had been named, they were great-aunt and great-uncle to Connor, Gracie and the rest of the Bravo siblings. Dante had always liked them. Daffy was charming and sweet. Percy could tell you way more than you ever needed to know about the history of Valentine Bay.

Once the food had been served, the speeches began. Dante's dad and mom got up and congratulated the happy couple, as did Percy and then Daffy. There was plenty of wine to toast Aly and Connor's reunion. The two had never looked happier—with each other and with their adorable baby.

Dante spotted Gracie several tables away. She sat with Harper, Hailey and their older sister, Aislinn. Aislinn's husband, Jax Winter, had the chair beside his wife. There were also three guys he didn't recognize. The sight of those guys had irritation prickling through him. Wasn't this supposed to be a family party?

Daffy Valentine, who sat on his left, said, "Dante. I understand our Gracie has moved into a little guest cabin on your property."

He turned and met her twinkly blue eyes. "She wanted to get out on her own and the cabin was empty."

The network of wrinkles on Daffy's face deepened as she smiled. "That was so kind of you."

"Gracie's a good friend."

"Oh, I have no doubt. She has such a big heart." Daffy patted his arm with her perfectly manicured, age-spotted hand. "And I am trusting you to treat her well."

What was he supposed to say to that? Had Gracie told the old woman what was going on between them?

"No," said Daffy, as though answering the question he hadn't asked aloud. "Grace has never said a word to me about you. But I have eyes, young man, and I know how to use them."

Okay, fine. The old lady had him pegged. He respected that. Enough that he refused to lie to her face. Feeling sheepish, he asked, "Am I that obvious?"

Daffy smiled wider and patted his arm again.

* * *

After dinner and dessert, there was dancing. Dante danced with Aly, with his mother, with each of his daughters and his niece Heather. Every time he looked for Gracie, she was dancing with someone else. He hesitated to cut in, mostly because he wanted her in his arms way too much and every time he spotted her with another guy, he felt like a jealous boyfriend who might just lose his cool.

And who did he think he was kidding? He *was* a jealous boyfriend—the secret kind. And being a secret boyfriend at a party like this? It seriously sucked.

After sunset, various family members gathered up groups of kids for sleepovers at predesignated houses. Natalie and Nicole, looking worn out and happy and clutching the gift bags Aly had given them, went home with Dante's brother Tony and Tony's wife, Lisa, and their boys.

Dante shouldn't be so glad to see his own children go, but he was feeling a little nuts watching all the couples looking so happy together. He wanted time with Gracie and so far, he'd gotten none.

He felt resentful that she hadn't sat with him during dinner, at the same time knowing damn well that if she sat with him, Daffy Valentine wouldn't be the only one to put two and two to-gether. Gracie's brothers would probably get over-protective of her. At the very least, Dante would never hear the end of questions about where he and Grace were going as a couple and how serious was it, anyway? His mom would be over the moon with happiness, already planning the wedding.

Uh-uh. None of that, thanks.

But damn it, he wanted a dance. If he could just keep his absurd and pointless jealousy under con-trol, a dance was no biggie. It was totally within the bounds of their very real friendship and family connection that he would ask Grace for a dance—during which he could not only hold her in his arms, but would also pull out all the stops to get her agreement to spending the whole night with him. Tonight. Again. At last.

He stood on the edge of the big flagstone patio that served as the dance floor, his eyes on the silky-haired blonde in the blue dress as she danced with one of those unknown interlopers who'd shared her table at dinner. As the song ended, Dante stepped up. He was waiting right behind the other guy when the last guitar note faded off.

Gracie saw him—how could she help it? He was three feet away from her and staring straight at her. Over the other guy's shoulder, she beamed him a smile of pure devilment. Because she knew she made him crazy and she found that humorous.

In the end, he had to tap that fool who had hold of her on the shoulder.

"Oh!" the guy said, like it had never occurred to him that at some point, he would have to let go of her. "Sure…" He gave Gracie a nod. "Thanks, Grace."

"Ray." Gracie gave him a smile as she stepped into Dante's arms. Now that he was holding her, he felt better about everything. The music started up again. It was a fast song, but Dante kept his arms around her anyway, wasting no time dancing her away from her previous partner. "Who was that guy?"

She snort-laughed, like he was just the funniest thing. "Nice to see you, too."

Was he coming on too strong? Probably. It was a problem he had. He took things way too seriously—even this damn secret fling of theirs that was supposed to be just for fun. Drawing a slow, deep breath, he toned down the attitude. "I was only, you know, wondering…"

"Ray Danvers. He works for Jax." Aislinn's husband owned a horse ranch on the Youngs River not far from Astoria. "Ray's a nice guy."

"I'll bet." He danced her out toward the perimeter of the patio.

"It's a fast song, in case you didn't notice," she razzed him. "What *are* you doing?"

Probably blowing our cover all to hell. So what? Right at this moment, he didn't even care. He pulled her closer. "I missed you. I want to talk to you alone and I want to do that now." He grabbed her hand.

She laughed again, but she didn't pull away. Instead, she let him lead her down the nearest garden path. In-ground lights led the way from one winding stone walkway to another. He followed those walkways, branching left and then right, pulling her deeper into the lush shelter of the estate's gardens.

"Where are we going?" she asked as the stone path took another turn and they entered a small pocket of shadowed greenery hemmed in by tall trees and accented in the far corner with a narrow, rustic-looking gardener's shed. The music sounded far away now.

"This'll do." He pulled her around in front of him and backed her up until she reached the shed. Her eyes burned into his and her breath came fast. Apparently, he wasn't the only one glad they were finally alone. He braced his hands on either side of her head and bent to steal a quick, hard kiss. "Nicole and Natalie went home with Tony and Lisa. Spend the night with me tonight."

She lifted those long, pale arms and rested them on his shoulders. "I was hoping you might say that."

All of a sudden, the world was a beautiful place and he was a very happy man. "That's a yes?"

"Um, yeah." She sounded a little bit breathless. He liked her breathless. He liked it a lot. "That is a yes."

"Excellent." And he could not wait another second to kiss her. He bent his head and she lifted that plump mouth at the same time as he clasped her waist and slid his hands lower, until he cradled her perfect bottom. Once he had a good grip on her, he scooped her up off the ground.

With a hot little moan, she wrapped her arms and legs around him. Carefully, he braced her against the wall of the shed and deepened the already drowning kiss as her soft, sweet, delicious mouth opened so willingly for him.

"So good," she whispered as he lifted his mouth just enough to slant it the other way.

"The best…" He sank into her kiss again, his mind spinning, his body hard and hungry—to be alone, just the two of them, to get out of all these damn clothes. "It's been too long…"

"Secret flings." She made a cute little growling sound, nipped at his lower lip and raked her fingers up the back of his neck into his hair. "So inconvenient…"

"We'll have time tonight. I don't pick Nic and Nat up from Tony's until noon tomorrow."

"Good." She kissed the word into his mouth. "Very, very good…"

And then they stopped talking. Which was more than okay with him. He kissed her for the longest time, letting himself get lost in the feel of her wrapped all around him, her breasts so soft against his chest, the core of her pressing into his hardness. It was sheer agony of the most spectacular kind.

Until a man's voice directly behind him demanded, "Just what do you think you're doing with my little sister?"

Chapter Ten

Dante muttered an oath.

Gracie buried her face in the side of his throat. "Connor," she said glumly.

Dante stroked her silky hair, wanting to soothe her even though she seemed more disappointed than upset.

She braced her chin on his shoulder and said to the man behind him, "Go away, Connor." If Connor moved, Dante didn't hear it. There was only silence. Gracie whispered in his ear, "He's still there. Your sister's with him."

"It's okay," he promised her. What else was he going to say? Slowly and carefully, he eased Gracie to the ground. She landed lightly on her feet and gazed up at him, her eyes calm as the ocean on a clear, windless day, her skin translucent in the moonlight. He touched her smooth cheek and whispered, "You good?"

"Never better." She drew back her slim shoulders and smoothed the full skirt of her dress. He offered his hand and she took it. Together, they faced her brother, his lifelong best friend—the friend he'd beaten the crap out of when he first learned that Connor had been with *his* sister.

And really, to be fair, Connor had given as good as he got that day. Dante might have fractured one of Connor's fingers, but Connor had broken Dante's nose.

Right now, Connor was giving him some serious stink-eye, but at least he was restraining himself from throwing the first punch.

For Dante, it was a moment of uncomfortable truth. He recalled his boundless fury at Connor all those years ago for daring to get something going with Aly.

And right now? He had no idea what Connor might be thinking. Probably nothing all that good.

Back at the party, the band was playing the Avett Brothers' "No Hard Feelings." Gracie's hand was cool and soft in his and he felt like crap for putting her in this position. Still, whatever happened next, he was glad for every moment he'd held her in his arms, for every night on the deck, just the two of them, under the moon, for the sweet, free sound of her laughter that always made him feel that the world was a better place than he'd ever realized before.

What happened next was that Aly snickered. "We knew there was something going on with you two. You're not fooling anyone."

Connor gazed at him steadily. "I meant what I said last month at Fisherman's Korner. We're good." At Dante's slow nod, Connor added, "But we couldn't resist giving you a little taste of your own medicine."

Aly taunted, "Tell me, big brother. How does it feel to have your best friend all up in your face because you had the nerve to get together with his sister?"

Dante considered the question and then answered it honestly. "Not so great." He was equal parts embarrassed at his own past behavior and resentful that his sister and brother-in-law had interrupted a completely amazing stolen moment with Gracie.

"Okay, you guys." Gracie waved a dismissing hand. "Whatever your point was, I'm guessing you've made it."

Connor said, "He gives you trouble, Gracie, you come to me. I'll set him straight." He was only half joking, and Dante got that message loud and clear.

"Move on," commanded Gracie.

Aly slipped her hand in Connor's. "You kids have fun, now." Together, they set off down the path.

Dante waited until they'd disappeared around the next bend before turning to the woman beside him and tipping her soft chin up with a finger. "So much for the families not finding out."

She gazed up at him with the strangest look on her beautiful face—a sad look? He wasn't sure. She shrugged. "What happened at Fisherman's Korner?"

"I apologized to your brother for being an ass way back when he and Aly first got together."

"Wow. About time, huh?"

"Past time."

She studied his face for several seconds before asking, "So, then. What now?"

He snaked an arm around her waist and pulled her up nice and tight against him. "Right now, all I want to do is get you home alone."

Dante got back to the house first, put the truck in the garage and then stood out in the driveway to wait for her, impatience thrumming through him with every eager beat of his heart.

Finally, her little SUV turned in and rolled to a stop a few feet from where he stood.

She leaned out the window with a silvery laugh. "How am I going to park if you're in the way?"

"Come to my place."

Her eyes shone so bright. "Will do."

She parked in her space by the cabin. He met her midway between his house and her car. She paused and gazed up at him through the moon-dappled shadows made by the tall trees. "You're blocking the driveway again."

He couldn't wait to kiss her. "Come here."

With a husky giggle, she swayed toward him. He took her by her silky bare shoulders and pulled her into his waiting arms.

Nothing compared to this—holding Gracie. It never got old. Every touch, every kiss, every breathless little sigh was a new revelation. Now he had her close, it kind of didn't matter what happened next. He could have stood there in the driveway beneath the giant trees, kissing her, holding her, kissing her some more.

She was the one who finally pulled away—but only far enough to ask against his parted lips, "Are we going to stand here all night, just kissing and kissing?"

"Yes." He caught her lower lip between his teeth and pulled on it gently.

She laughed and kissed him some more, turning in his arms at the same time. Still kissing, they started walking toward the house.

"You want anything?" He asked as he ushered her in through the side door.

"Just you…"

And they were kissing again. He guided her backward, his mouth fused to hers, through the mudroom, the kitchen, the living area and on down the hall to his room.

"Where's Owen?" she asked as he untied those little bows at her shoulders.

"At the dog sitter's. He's staying over—and I really like this dress. Mostly because I've been dreaming all night of getting you out of it." He peeled down the front. She was naked underneath. "No bra…"

"It's built in."

He pretended to frown. "And here I was thinking you went without one just to drive me crazy."

"*Did* I drive you crazy?"

He bent close and caught a pretty little nipple lightly between his teeth. When she moaned, he smiled against her soft, pale flesh. "You have no idea…"

* * *

Much later, satisfied and at peace with the world and everyone in it at last, holding her close, skin to skin, he couldn't help wishing they could just do this every night. Be together, in and out of bed, whenever they felt like it.

No sneaking around.

And why not, really? Why couldn't they have more?

He asked the question of himself—and automatically, the answers came to him. He'd tried having more, making a family, sticking with it no matter what. And look where that had gone. He was no good at the true-love-forever thing. He didn't want his daughters' lives disrupted, couldn't stand for them to develop a close relationship with Gracie and then have it all go to hell.

And what about Gracie? She was young and fresh and ready for anything. The last thing she needed was to tie herself down to a grumpy cop with a ready-made family…

She shifted against him, lifting her head, bracing up on an elbow to gaze down at him. "What?"

He caught a lock of that pretty pale hair and rubbed it between his fingers. "Not a thing."

She gave him that smile, the one that said he wasn't fooling her one bit. "Liar." But she said it softly, with affection, and then tucked her head beneath his chin again.

"Tired?"

She made a small, throaty sound in the affirmative.

He reached over and turned off the light.

"The guy is so hot." Erin took a contemplative sip of the white wine Grace had chosen to go with her chicken alfredo. "And those arms. Those shoulders…" Erin put down her wineglass long enough to kiss the tips of her fingers in a gesture of sheer appreciation.

Carrie tossed her head back with a moan. "Officer, cuff me now!"

No, Grace hadn't said a word to either of her girlfriends about her secret fling with Dante. But he'd been out on his deck grilling dinner when Carrie and Erin arrived. And Grace's BFFs loved nothing so much as discussing the do-ability of a good-looking man.

"I hope your secret boyfriend is something really special, because I can't believe you're not all over that." Erin sounded downright accusing. "I'm disappointed in you. I mean, you and Dante are friends and he's single. And *you're* single. He lives—what?—fifty yards from your front door?

You wouldn't even need your car to get to him. Talk about a missed opportunity."

"We are *so* disappointed in you." Carrie faked a sulky face.

"So sorry to let you down," Grace replied, sounding not the least apologetic. Really, she did feel a little bit guilty for not admitting that she was totally on top of the hot cop situation, both literally and figuratively. Because they *were* her friends and when it came to guys, the three of them had always confided in each other.

But Dante was such a private man. It seemed wrong to discuss their relationship—or whatever the heck she should call what they had—with her friends.

How had it become so complicated? She was constantly stewing over how she wanted more from Dante. And yet she still wasn't willing to take a chance and tell him how she felt.

A walking cliché. Oh, yes, she was. Friends with secret benefits! Terrific idea! What could possibly go wrong?

She just didn't want to talk about it. Not right now. There was nowhere to go with it except in a circle.

Erin leaned forward in her chair. "You're too quiet about this. And what is that look on your face?" She turned to Carrie as understanding dawned. "Do you see what I see?"

Carrie's eyes got wide. "Oh. My. God. I see it." She shifted her gaze to Grace and accused, "It is so on between you and the hot cop single dad."

Grace kept her mouth shut as she tried to decide how much to say.

"He's the one, isn't he?" demanded Erin. "He's the guy you're seeing that you're not telling us about."

"Wait," commanded Carrie.

"What?" asked Erin.

Carrie reached across the table and gave Grace's arm a squeeze. "If you don't want to talk about it, that's okay."

"Speak for yourself." Erin glared at Carrie. "Talking is *good*. She *needs* to talk about it."

Carrie held her ground. "Say the word. We'll shut up."

Erin threw up both hands. "I can't fight you both. Fine, Gracie. You don't want to talk about it, say the word and we won't."

"Much," smirked Carrie.

Grace bit her lip and shook her head. "There's not a lot to say. It's a temporary arrangement that we agreed to keep just between us."

"But now *we* know," said Carrie.

Grace blew out her cheeks with a hard breath. "You guys and Connor and Aly. And Harper and Hailey. And just possibly the rest of our families by now. Maybe others. I wouldn't be surprised."

"So as for the secret part," Carrie concluded for her. "You're saying not so much at this point."

"Essentially, yeah."

Erin said, "And *you* don't even care who knows— I mean, the secret thing is *his* deal?"

"Exactly. And even Dante's kind of accepted that the truth has gotten out."

"Is he pulling back from you, now that people know?"

"No."

"And *you* still want to be with *him*?"

"Yeah. I do. I really, really do."

"Then why are you wearing your sad face?"

"I'm not."

"You so are."

"You like him a lot?" Carrie suggested. "Maybe too much?"

Why deny it? "Yeah. And I don't think he's up for anything beyond what we have already."

"But *you* want more?" asked Erin softly.

Carrie was nodding. "Gracie. It's written all over your face."

"Yeah, well, I don't think I'm getting more."

"Oh, babes!" Erin cried as she and Carrie jumped from their chairs and surrounded her. Bending down, they hugged her from either side. Carrie stroked her hair and Erin patted her shoulder.

Carrie said, "Whatever you need, you just let us know."

"I love you guys," she whispered and hugged them back.

When they returned to their chairs, Erin announced, "Just for the record and then I'll leave it alone—he's an idiot if he walks away from you."

"I'll drink to that." Carrie emptied her glass.

The next morning at a little before eleven, Grace got a text from Dante. Want some company? The cabin? About noon?

She stared at her phone, a giant smile on her face. Her heart felt lighter as pure happiness filled her. Dante was coming over and everything was suddenly right with the world.

And that was when it hit her.

"I am in big trouble," she whispered to no one in particular. With a slow, careful sigh, she sank to the edge of the bed and set the phone on the old bureau next to it. "I've got it bad."

So bad. Worse every day. Stronger than liking

him a whole lot and longing to make it more. This was a huge deal, what she was feeling. This was…

Grace did not allow herself to think the forbidden word right then.

But it was there, nonetheless. A fiery ball of longing had tucked itself under her breastbone and become impossible to completely ignore.

This, with Dante, it was serious for her, way beyond anything she'd ever known. It wasn't going to just run its course. Dante wasn't Niall or Keegan or Paolo to her. He was her true friend and the man she wanted in her bed. The man she wanted to tell all her secrets to. The one she longed to turn to when things weren't working out, the one she wanted to be there for wherever, however, whenever he needed her.

And the girls…

Yes. Nicole and Natalie, too.

No, the girls didn't need her, exactly. Nic and Nat already had a good life. They actually seemed to enjoy both of their homes—with their mom and their stepdad in Portland *and* with Dante in Valentine Bay. They didn't *need* another parent, per se.

But they did like Grace and she liked them. A lot.

She could…add to the good they already had. She could make their time with their dad even better. She could take a little of the weight off Dante, help ferry them around, make dinner half the time. She could be there for the girly things, the hair braiding and the all-important search for just the right outfit for this or that event. She could lend an ear if either of them wanted to share a secret that only a woman might understand.

And yes, those were all things that would get handled anyway, without her. The girls had a great mom and a loving, attentive dad. They had everything they needed to get a good start in life.

All Grace could offer them was more...

More could be good for them and for her.

More could be excellent.

If Dante would only let her in.

Grace fell back across the bed and stared blindly at the rustic beam ceiling above.

So, then. The girls would be going home in less than a week. She wouldn't approach Dante about her deepening feelings until after they were gone. If he turned her down, Nicole and Natalie didn't need to be there while the breakup was happening.

On the bureau, her phone buzzed with another text.

She sat up long enough to grab it and flopped back across the mattress again.

So is that a no?

"Dante." Just saying his name out loud sent a sweet little shiver racing along the surface of her skin. She pressed the phone to her chest and reminded herself to count her blessings. However it all shook out in the end, right now was amazing. In less than an hour, she would have his arms around her—and she could not wait.

She really had it bad for him. So very bad. Noon, you said?

Yeah.

I'm here at the cabin. C U then.

He arrived right on time. They spent a perfect hour in her bed.

When he left, she stood at the door and watched him drive away in his cruiser. Her body felt relaxed, thoroughly satisfied. But her heart was a big ball of longing.

For everything. The L-word from his lips, a future to share with him.

One step at a time, though. She was fine with that, with taking it slow.

But in the end, she did want it all. With him.

She wanted all the things he'd made it painfully clear he would never give.

The next night, she joined him and the girls for dinner at his place. When Nat and Nic went to bed, Grace stayed for a couple of hours. They sat out on the deck. With Owen snoozing at their feet, they watched the wisps of clouds drifting past the moon, spoke of inconsequential things and somehow managed to keep their hands off each other.

Thursday and Friday, she worked six to closing and he couldn't get away at lunch either day.

Saturday morning, Gracie was still sound asleep when someone knocked on the door. She peeled one eye open long enough to wave her hand over her cell phone and see that it was 7:25. She'd arrived home at three this morning. Four hours and change did not add up to a good night's sleep.

She put the pillow over her head and hoped whoever it was would go away.

Another knock.

She dragged the pillow off her head. With her eyes scrunched shut, she shouted, "Come back later!"

Then she heard giggling. *Nicole and Natalie.*

A third knock, this one more tentative than the two before.

By then, she was awake enough to remember that this was the Saturday the girls returned to Portland. "Coming!" she shouted, and threw back the covers.

"We're sorry to wake you up," said Natalie when Grace opened the door.

"But we have to leave today," added Nicole.

"Come have breakfast with us," said Nat.

"Please," added Nic.

Owen, at their feet, panted eagerly up at Grace and beat his tail against the boards of the front step.

Grace felt kind of forlorn. "Can't you just stay and never go?" She made a pouty face.

"We will miss you." Nic gazed up at her through serious brown eyes a lot like her dad's. "But we live in Portland, too."

"I understand, I guess. And I will miss *you*," Grace replied. "And yes, I would love to have breakfast with you. I'll be over in ten minutes."

When she got to Dante's, the girls had already set the table and Dante had crisp bacon on a serving platter and tall stacks of pancakes ready. Grace poured herself a cup of coffee and sat down with them.

Nic and Nat talked nonstop—about how they hated to leave their Valentine Bay friends and cousins, but they needed to get back to Portland, where one of their friends was having a birthday party next weekend. And they'd been invited by another friend to the big water park an hour south of Portland in McMinnville this coming Wednesday.

Dante seemed kind of quiet. Grace sensed he was already missing them.

Too soon, breakfast was over. Grace helped clear the table and then carried a couple of suitcases out to the crew cab as they loaded up to go.

Finally, it was time for goodbyes.

Gracie hugged Nic first. "I already miss you."

"Me too." Nic's small arms squeezed her tighter.

"We'll see you in two weeks and then in September," Nat promised.

"They're here for just the weekend in mid-August," Dante explained kind of gruffly. "And then I'll go get them for Labor Day."

"I can't wait," Grace said, reaching for Nat.

Nat hugged her good and hard and then tipped her head up to meet Grace's eyes. "Be extra nice to Owen while we're gone."

"He misses us so much," Nic explained with a sad little sigh.

"I will help your dad take really good care of

him," Grace vowed. "In fact, I'll take him back to the cabin with me now. How's that?"

"That would be good." Nat nodded up at her. "He won't have to be alone."

A moment later, the girls were climbing into their booster seats and buckling up.

Dante got in behind the wheel. He leaned out the window. "I'll be back in a few hours. Any chance you'll be around?"

She ached for him. He always tried to be so tough. But really, he had a heart of pure mush and it was so painfully obvious how much he hated to see his daughters go. "I'll be here."

With Owen sitting at her feet, Grace waved them off. She felt a bit teary eyed, watching them go. It gave her a deeper sense of how hard it must be for Dante every time they returned to their other home in Portland.

Four hours later, she and Dante were in her bed wearing nothing but a matched pair of satisfied grins.

He wrapped a big arm around her and pulled her close against his side. She snuggled in with her head on his broad chest.

"I hate when they go." He idly stroked a hand down the bare skin of her arm.

"I noticed." She brushed a kiss on the hot, muscled flesh just above his left nipple.

Smoothing her hair out of the way, he trailed a finger along the side of her throat. "But I could get used to having more time like this with you, to being able to kiss you on the back deck without thinking about who might be watching."

I don't care who might be watching, she thought as frustration welled within her. *I don't care who knows about you and me. I want Nic and Nat to know that we have something good together. I really do. And we need to talk about that.*

Stacking her hands on his chest, she rested her chin on them, captured his gaze—and had absolutely no idea where to start.

I want more from you, Dante.

Ugh.

You could kiss me on the back deck whenever you wanted if we just tell the girls that we're more than friends.

No.

Where are we going, you and I, Dante?

Yuck.

It all sounded pitiful and needy and wrong inside her own head.

Clearly, more thought was required before she broached this particular subject with him.

He pressed his palm to her cheek. "What is it?"

Nope. Not going there. Not until she'd at least figured out what she wanted to say.

"This." Lifting up, she pressed her mouth to his.

He made a low, pleasured sound against her parted lips and dipped his tongue inside.

After that, they didn't need words.

A good thing, too, because she sure hadn't found the right ones yet.

With the girls gone, they did have more time alone together. In the next week, they spent two lunchtimes in her bed. And on Monday and Wednesday, when neither of them had to work at night, they shared dinner on the deck and she stayed the night at his house.

Thursday morning before she left him to get ready to open at the Sea Breeze, he asked her if maybe she could get Saturday night off. "I want to take you to dinner."

Her heart soared.

A date. An actual date. Out in public where anyone might see them.

This was progress, right?

But then he added, "I know this great seafood place on the river in Astoria."

Her soaring heart crashed and burned.

Astoria. Of course. Where the chances were pretty small they would ever run into anyone they knew.

Yeah. It was time. She needed to find the damn words, to tell him what she wanted from him.

However. An actual date was a step in the right direction. She decided to be glad about that.

"I'll check with Ingrid," she said.

Ingrid gave her the night off. She and Dante had dinner out like any regular couple. It was a good night. They laughed and talked about their families and their jobs. They shared a dessert and whispered together the way people in actual relationships do. And then they went back to his house and he gave her lots of deep kisses and more than one orgasm.

The next week, it was pretty much the same. They got together whenever both of their schedules allowed. She loved every minute she had with him. She didn't want anything to change.

She just wanted to *not* be a secret. Yeah. That would do it for her for now.

That Friday, she had the closing shift at the Sea Breeze and she slept nice and late on Saturday morning.

Nicole and Natalie arrived while she was still sleeping.

They woke her the same way they had the day they left—with giggles at her front door. She let them and Owen in. They stayed for an hour, laughing and chattering, bringing her up-to-date on their lives in Portland and their trip to Wings and Waves Waterpark, which had a giant wave pool and the coolest tube slides ever.

Then Dante appeared. He hustled them off to their grandmother's house for a barbecue.

After they left, Grace sat on the old sofa in the cabin and tried not to feel hurt that Dante hadn't invited her to go with them. Because how could he invite her? If Dante took her to a Santangelo family get-together, everyone would start wondering if the two of them were more than friends.

Well, they *were* more than friends. A lot more, at least as far as she was concerned.

And it wasn't working for her that he didn't seem willing to actually acknowledge that.

With a groan, she bent forward and put her head in her hands. Really, she had no right to go blaming Dante for not giving her what she hadn't even asked for. She needed to stop being a big baby about this, to either tell him she wanted to change the rules, or let it be and enjoy the ride for as long as it lasted.

Up until this thing with Dante, she'd always been an enjoy-the-ride kind of girl.

Not anymore, though.

She wanted to *be* with him and she wanted the world to know that she was his and he was hers.

Never, ever had she felt this way before.

And it really brought her spirits down that he seemed perfectly happy to keep things just as they were.

Sunday, the girls came over about noon. She went back to the main house with them and Dante fixed lunch for the four of them. Then she was treated to a karaoke performance that included just about every Disney song ever written.

Too soon, it was time to pack up the truck again. Dante would drive the girls to meet their mother, come back home just long enough to change clothes and then head for the station house, dropping Owen at the dog sitter's on the way.

Gracie hugged the girls goodbye and waved as they drove off. Missing them already, she decided to cheer herself up by going to dinner at Daniel's.

At the house on Rhinehart Hill, she played with her nieces and nephews, spent some time with her sisters and just generally felt better about everything with her family around her. She didn't see Dante until the next morning.

She was lying in bed, half-awake, at a little after seven, thinking of getting up and making some coffee when he tapped on her door. "Gracie?"

Of course, her hopeless heart beat faster and she couldn't stop the happy smile that spread over her face. "Coming!" She rolled out of bed and went to let him in.

"There you are." He looked at her with those melty dark eyes and suddenly nothing else in the world mattered as much as the fact that he was standing there on her front step, in jeans and a T-shirt, his hair still wet from a shower.

"Did you just get home from work?"

He nodded. "God. You look good."

"Please. I look like the bed I just rolled out of."

"You're beautiful." He stepped over the threshold, crowding her backward.

"Just come right on in, why don't you?"

"Thanks. I will." He reached for her. Wrapping a big arm around her waist, he pulled her up close. "I've been thinking all night about getting my hands on you." His mouth came down on hers before she had a chance to warn him about morning breath.

And really, morning breath? Who cares? Nothing mattered but his kiss and his arms so tight around her—that, and getting prone.

Or maybe up against the wall.

Or straddling him on the sofa…

He had her cami and sleep shorts off in seconds flat as she tore at his shirt and whipped off his belt. It took him a moment to get out of his boots and socks. And then he shoved down his jeans and boxers and he was every bit as naked as she was.

They fell on each other, moaning.

The next hour went by in a hot haze of pleasure. Even in a one-room cabin, there were so many surfaces to explore. They ended up in the bed, their arms wrapped around each other.

As her heartbeat settled into a slower rhythm, she nipped the side of his neck and whispered, "Coffee. I need it. Now."

He held her closer. "No. I want you here."

She laughed and playfully shoved at his broad, bare chest. Reluctantly, he let her go. Bracing his head on his hand, he watched, grinning, as she darted around grabbing her rumpled cami and sleep shorts off the floor and yanking them back on.

She was at the kitchen counter loading up the coffee maker when he came up behind her and eased his warm arms around her again.

Smoothing her hair back, he nuzzled her neck.

"I came by last night before I went to work, but missed you," he said in her ear.

"I went to Sunday dinner at Daniel's."

He caught her earlobe between his teeth and teased at it lightly, causing a cascade of shivers to skate down her neck and over her jaw. "Were Aly and Connor there?"

"Mmm-hmm."

"They warn you off me?"

She pushed the brew button and turned in his hold. He'd pulled on his jeans, which hung a little low without his belt, revealing V-lines a fitness model might envy. She stuck her thumbs in the belt loops on either side of his hard hips and tugged him a fraction closer. "You were not mentioned. By either your sister or my brother."

He guided a swatch of hair behind her ear, his eyes kind of guarded. "What about your aunt Daffodil?"

"What about her?"

"Was she there?"

"Yeah." She looked at him sideways. "Why?"

His shrug was too offhand. "At Aly and Connor's party three weeks ago, Daffy and Percy sat with me and the girls. Daffy mentioned you, said she was trusting me to treat you right. I got the impression she'd noticed that I couldn't keep my eyes off you."

It pleased her no end to picture him blowing his cover because he couldn't stop staring at her. "Aunt Daffy's a very perceptive woman."

"Did she say anything to you last night—about us? Give you any strange looks?"

"Nope. We shared a hug when I got there and she didn't say a word about you. As for strange looks she might have sent my way, I didn't see any." And this seemed like the perfect moment to make her position clear on this subject. "The truth is, I don't really care what anyone says about you and me, Dante. And I don't care what they know, either."

He ran a slow finger down the side of her neck and then outward to her shoulder, where he idly fiddled with the lace strap of her cami. "The way I see it, if Daffy and Aly and Connor and everyone else in town have decided to just keep their mouths shut about us, that works for me."

A sharp spike of irritation twisted in her stomach at his words. Okay, yeah. He was a very private man. But she was so tired of being his sexy little secret—or if not a secret, something no one was supposed to talk about.

It was way past time she made her position clear.

But she really didn't want to get into some deep discussion about where they were "going" and how she wanted "more" from him than he'd said he could give. She'd been racking her brain to come up with a light, evenhanded approach to this issue.

And then, as she stood there at the counter with him so close she could melt right into him, it came to her—the perfect way to find out what she needed to know. "So I've been thinking…"

He lowered his head a fraction. Those fine lips hovered just inches from hers. "I really love the way you think."

Maybe not about this, though. "You know, there's a family dinner at Daniel's pretty much every Sunday. We all have an open invitation."

He tipped up her chin with a finger and brushed his mouth across hers. "I'm aware." He kissed her again. "You taste so good. I can never get enough of you. Let's go back to bed."

She slipped her thumbs from his belt loops and pressed her hands against his beautiful, bare chest. "Dante, listen to me."

The sex fog in his dark eyes cleared a little and

a tiny frown drew down between his thick black eyebrows. "I'm listening."

She stared up at him, keeping her gaze steady and true. "I want you to come with me next Sunday to Daniel's for the Bravo family dinner."

He blinked, a dead giveaway. She knew she wouldn't like whatever he said next. She was right. He stepped back an inch or so. "Gracie. If I go to Daniel's with you, they're all going to think we're together."

Because we are together.

That little spike of annoyance in her belly? All at once, it was a spear shoved clean through her. "So then, that's a no?"

"I thought we had an agree—"

"Just say it, please."

"Gracie…"

"Say it."

"No. I think it's a bad idea. I think we really need to keep things—"

"Shh." She stopped his words with the gentle touch of her fingers to his lips. "I understand," she said softly. "You don't need to say another word."

"We did agree from the first—"

"Yes, we did. I get it. It's fine." Lifting on tiptoe, she replaced her fingertips with her open mouth.

It was a wet kiss, a long kiss, slow and hot and full of sexual promise, a kiss that said everything he needed to know at that moment. Everything about right now.

And nothing more.

Because right now was what they had and he didn't want more.

Okay, yeah. Maybe she ought to do the adult thing—communicate. Maybe she should talk it out with him, tell him what her sisters had said to tell him, that she needed more or she was moving on.

But ultimatums weren't her style. And it was all just too sad and depressing. Not to mention, it hurt. A lot. She'd been agonizing over this for weeks now. The longing had kind of worn her down. It just shouldn't be this hard with a guy, should it?

But it *was* hard. The hardest thing ever.

And she knew why.

She felt so much for him. More than for Joey or Randy in high school. More than for Niall or Keegan or Paolo. She might as well just admit it—to herself, at least.

She'd fallen in love with this man.

And that scared her to death. Especially now

she fully understood that her love was going no-where.

She'd fallen in love with Dante Santangelo and he didn't want anything more than great sex for as long as it lasted—oh, and her friendship. He wanted that, too.

And she wanted *his* friendship. Maybe. Eventually. If she ever got over him.

She just saw no point in humiliating herself. He'd made it way clear he wouldn't let her—or anyone—in. He was never going to the love place.

"Gracie…" He said her name with real feeling. With need and affection, with searing desire. Like she was everything to him, like she carried his heart inside her, precious, cherished. Protected. Safe.

Yeah, it was a lie, but such a perfect, beautiful lie. She needed to indulge that lie.

One last time.

Scooping her up, he took her back to the bed and laid her down on the tangled sheets.

She reached up her arms to him, twined them around his neck and pulled him down to her, so close. So tender. So exactly right.

Just the way a last time ought to be.

When he came into her, she rocked him slow and sweet, legs and arms locked around him, feeling him within her, so hot and deep, as their kiss went on and on. He tasted of wonder and pleasure and all the love he refused to give her.

But it was beautiful, anyway. He gave what he could. And as she moved with him, so tight, so close, she knew he had no idea that she was letting him go.

Afterward, she cooked him eggs with sausage. She made sourdough toast with marionberry jam. As they ate, she asked him about his work schedule.

"I'm off for the rest of the day," he said, and she knew he was filling her in on his schedule so they could figure out when and how they might next hook up. "I'm going to get some sleep. And I told my dad I would help him haul some stuff to the dump. So there goes my afternoon."

"Your mom'll want you to stay for dinner."

"Probably." His eyes made promises she wasn't going to be available to help him keep. "But I'll be home by eight, eight thirty. How 'bout you?"

She sipped her coffee and then shook her head. "I promised Cassie and Erin I'd be over for dinner. We tend to run late when we get together."

Now he was looking rueful. "Tomorrow, I'm pulling a twelve-hour shift. Six a.m. to six p.m."

"And I've got to work tomorrow night."

"That's inconvenient."

She gave him a little nod for an answer.

"I'll miss you." He said it tenderly.

She replied in kind. "I'll miss you, too." And she would.

So very much.

The next evening, Dante picked up Owen from the sitter and got home at six thirty.

He'd had an hour free at lunch and sent Gracie a text hoping maybe they could steal a little time at the cabin. She'd never texted back. And by now, she would be mixing drinks at the Sea Breeze.

Tomorrow, he didn't go in until four in the afternoon, so he had a good chance of seeing her tomorrow morning—late, so she could get enough sleep.

As he unlocked his front door, he was thinking he would send her another text just to check in, make sure everything was okay with her. There had been that rough moment yesterday, when she'd invited him to Sunday dinner at Daniel's and he'd turned her down.

She'd seemed okay afterwards, though.

More than okay. She'd kissed him and that had led to another totally satisfying interval in bed. She'd even made him breakfast after and he'd been reassured that they were back on the same page about everything.

He pushed the door inward. That was when he saw the plain white envelope on the floor. It had his name on it. He bent to pick it up as Owen went around him, headed for the kitchen.

When he peeled back the flap, he found a single folded sheet of paper and the key to the cabin.

Chapter Eleven

Dante,
When this crazy, wonderful thing started
with us, we agreed it would last until one of
us called it off. And that's what this is—me,
calling it off. Thank you for the cottage. I've
loved living there. You really came through
when I needed a hand. Take care.
Gracie

His gut twisting and his heart beating a ragged
rhythm under his breastbone, Dante stood in the
open doorway and read the note through five times.
Take care?

That was it?

That was all he got?

After everything they'd had, she thought she could just scribble a quick note and give back the key?

He stuck the key in his pocket and whipped out his phone to call her and tell her in no uncertain terms that a damn note wasn't enough. Not by a long shot. They needed to talk.

They needed to work this out. She couldn't just run away like some irresponsible kid. She couldn't just…

The indignant thought died unfinished.

Because damn it, yes. She could. Those *were* the terms. He'd set them. He'd *agreed* with them. He'd really thought the terms were a good idea at the time, reasonable and clear. So simple and forthright.

He was an idiot.

And he should have known, shouldn't he?

Yesterday morning, when she'd asked him to Daniel's, he should have recognized the invitation for what it was, should have understood that she was saying she wanted more.

Should have figured out that if he turned her down, he very well might lose her.

His hand was shaking. *Both* hands. He glanced

from one to the other, ordering the shaking to stop and the aching emptiness in his chest to fill up with acceptance.

But acceptance was not happening.

Crumpling her note into a tight little ball, he let it fall to the floor. He dropped his phone on the entry table and went to the living area, where he flopped down on the sofa and shut his eyes.

There was no point in calling her. She'd made her position crystal clear, given him exactly what they'd agreed on.

A tidy, easy ending. No drama. Quick and clean.

He should be grateful. It was just about the best end he could have hoped for.

If only he was ready for it to end.

If only he hadn't started to doubt that he'd *ever* be ready to have Gracie walk away from him.

He lay there with his eyes closed, wishing he could just fall asleep and forget everything.

Didn't happen. Several minutes crept by.

And then Owen whined and licked the back of his hand.

He got up, fed the dog, made a sandwich and ate it standing at the kitchen window, looking out at the graveled driveway that wound into the evergreens and the cabin, barely visible back in the trees.

Owen whined at him again. The dog sat by his left foot, gazing up at him hopefully.

"She's gone," he said flatly. "She moved out today—apparently."

Another whine, the sound somehow more hopeful than ever.

"What? You need to go over there and see for yourself?"

That brought a short bark in the affirmative and three hard smacks of Owen's tail against the floor.

"Okay, then. Have it your way." He turned for the slider, Owen right behind him.

When they reached the cabin, he almost changed his mind. He didn't want to go in there and see all the ways she'd left him behind.

But then Owen whined at him again and he stuck the key in the lock.

Inside, it was pretty much as he expected. Her bed was gone. So was the chest of drawers she'd brought with her. The drawers of the other bureau were empty. No sexy satin and pretty lace, no naughty pleasure toys.

She'd cleaned out the fridge and taken the food she'd bought from the cupboards. The bathroom still smelled faintly of her bodywash and shampoo, but the medicine cabinet was empty.

When he returned to the main room, Owen was

curled up in the doggy bed she'd bought for him, his long face resting on his favorite chew toy. He looked up at Dante without lifting his head, his caramel eyes glum and faintly accusing.

"I don't even know where she went," he said to the dog, who just closed his eyes and chuffed out a heavy sigh. "Maybe back to Daniel's…"

Not that it mattered. Wherever she was, she didn't want him there. She'd made her point and he needed to let her go.

And he would. He'd get on with his life and let her get on with hers.

Alternately furious and bleakly resigned, Dante somehow managed to get through that night, the next day and eight hours of work.

He got home at three in the morning and tried to sleep. Mostly, he stared at the dark ceiling overhead and punched at his pillow a lot, trying to get comfortable, trying not to think of silver-blond hair, sea-blue eyes, a wicked laugh and sweet pink lips.

There was no point in going after her. He had nothing to offer her. He was set in his ways, not going to change, didn't have whatever it took to make the love thing work. The best thing he could do for her was to leave her the hell alone.

But at nine that morning, as he stared out the window over the sink, sipping coffee without really tasting it, he finally broke.

He called her.

It went straight to voicemail.

Miserable, disbelieving and angry that she wouldn't even take his damn call, he barked out a message.

Grace sat at the kitchen table in the cottage she now shared with Harper and Hailey, who had left at a little after eight to head over to the Valentine Bay Theater where they would be staging their next theatrical extravaganza.

The phone was right there on the table beside her. She watched it light up with Dante's name and she sent it to voicemail. Maybe he would leave a message, maybe not.

When the voicemail icon appeared and the phone gave an annoying beep, she set down her coffee cup and shifted her gaze to stare blindly at the cupboards above the sink. It hurt so much, being away from him.

She missed him—missed everything about him. The cloves-and-cedar scent of his skin, his reluctant smile, the proud jut of his strong cheekbones. His touch and his voice and his kisses…

It was awful, this being in love with Dante. Leave it to her to fall for a man who claimed outright he was bad at relationships and wouldn't be having one ever again.

She didn't want to talk to him and she wasn't going to talk to him. No way. There was no point. Rising, she refilled her coffee cup. For a minute or two, she stood at the counter, glaring at her phone, waffling about whether to check that voicemail or not.

Her constant longing for the mere sound of his voice won out. She took her cup back to the table and autodialed her voicemail.

His message was short and straight to the point. "What the hell, Gracie? We need to talk." He sounded really pissed.

Which was in no way her problem.

For another three or four minutes, she sat there stewing—aching to call him back, reminding herself that she'd already decided she wouldn't.

Finally, she gave in to her own hopeless longing and texted him. I've moved in with my sisters. She typed in the address of the cottage. I'm here until 2 p.m. You're welcome to stop by.

His response was instantaneous: On my way.

"Great," she muttered angrily, her silly heart beating so fast she imagined it leaping into her throat and right out her mouth, hitting the floor with a wet slapping sound, then flopping around desperately like a landed fish.

He would be here any minute.

Jumping up, she ran to her bedroom. Stripping out of her sleep shorts and Reed College T-shirt, she ran for the bathroom, where she brushed her teeth, splashed water on her face, put on deodorant and mascara and combed her hair.

What to wear?

God. Was she pathetic or what?

She did know him, after all. This wasn't a reunion. He was going to get all up in her grill about the way she'd left him and then remind her that it was all for the frickin' best.

Really, why did she have to go and fall in love with him? There were good guys in the world who actually *wanted* someone to love and cherish and bring home to the family.

She needed…sexy underwear.

Even though there was no way he was going to see it. He could crawl on his knees across a sea of broken glass swearing to love her forever, vowing never to leave her in a million years and to accompany her to dinner at Daniel's this coming Sunday—and he still wasn't getting a look at what she had under her clothes.

Not today, anyway.

It took a good three minutes of pawing around in her lingerie suitcase to decide on the perfect pair of lace-trimmed cobalt-blue satin cheekies and the bra to match. She put on the undies and then went to the dresser to whip out her best secret weapon: the faded, tattered jean shorts that showed way more than they should every time she bent over. Paired with a too-tight T-shirt and brass-riveted flip-flops with a cute bowtie detail, she was ready to face the emotionally unavailable man of her dreams.

And pigtails. Dante couldn't get enough of her in pigtails. And he wasn't going to get enough. In fact, he was getting *nothing* of her.

Not today.

She zipped back into the bathroom and braided her hair.

The front door buzzer sounded just as she snapped the elastic around the tail of the second braid. She smoothed her too-tight T-shirt and went to let him in.

One look at him standing there outside the door of the screened porch and all her false bravado fled. He looked tired. And sad.

And that broke her heart even worse than having to leave him because she wanted more and he wouldn't go there.

She pushed open the door.

He didn't step forward, but just stood there on the step looking her up and down. When he finally met her eyes again, she felt the pull of him so strongly. Her belly hollowed out and everything inside her burned.

"Now, that's just cruel." His voice was deliciously rough and low.

She flipped one of her pigtails back over her shoulder. "Yeah. Sorry. I was feeling kind of bitter. A little sexual torture seemed like a good idea."

He almost smiled. But not quite. "Let me in so we can talk?"

She considered his request. The thing was, she wanted him so much and there were beds and a couch in the house—not to mention all manner of other possible surfaces where they might get up to stuff she wasn't going to do with him. "How about a walk on the beach?"

He stuck his hands in the pockets of his black jeans and nodded. "Yeah. That'd be good."

Much like Dante's house and the cabin she missed a lot, the cottage was perched on a hill above a section of beach. She led him along the trail that led to the edge of the cliff and then down in a series of switchbacks to the sand.

He took off his boots and socks and rolled the

cuffs of his jeans. She slipped off her sandals. They went on across the sand until they reached the shore where the cold, foamy edges of the waves lapped at their toes.

It was nice, for a minute or two, just walking together along the wet sand, a gentle wind blowing, the air misty and cool. She wished he would take her hand—and then reminded herself that if he did, she would only pull away.

Finally, stopping and turning to face her, he got down to it. "I didn't want you to go. You know that, right?"

She pressed her lips together and gave him a nod.

"You just up and left—out of nowhere. I think I deserved more than a six-sentence note. Seriously, Gracie. The least you could have done was to break the news to me in person."

She really saw no other way to answer him but with brutal honesty. He deserved that. And so did she. "Dante, I'm in love with you." There. She'd said it. Too bad he flinched at the L-word, as though she'd slapped his face. "Don't look so shocked. You're here and you wanted to know, so I'm telling you. I love your daughters and I'm crazy about Owen. And I am in love with you."

"Gracie..." He started to reach for her.

She whipped up both hands, palms out. "Don't. Please."

He sucked in a slow breath through his nose and let his arm drop back to his side.

She made herself go on. "The thing is, I've never actually been in love before and I know I've handled this badly. But, um, we had a deal and you have made it painfully clear that, when it comes to love, you don't want to go there. You don't want a relationship. You don't want *more*." She lifted her hands and stacked them over her heart. "I do. I want it all with you. But I didn't ask for it all. I just wanted a step. That first step. I thought dinner at Daniel's could be that step, but maybe that was too much for you. If not, and I misjudged you and you're actually more willing than I believed, then please. Tell me what step you're willing to take. How far you're willing to go to get closer to me. Tell me your first step and we can take it from there."

"Gracie..." He looked stunned. Stricken. Totally wrecked.

"What?" Her voice had gone pleading now. "Just tell me. Just say it."

He swallowed, hard. "Thank you, for telling me."

She waited. But he said nothing more. "That's

it? That's all I get." It hurt, stabbed her to the heart all over again, to declare her love to him and have him dish out a reluctant thank-you in response. "You know what? There's no point in this. I want more and you don't and that's kind of the end of it, wouldn't you say?"

"You're right." His voice was so low, she wouldn't have heard him if she hadn't been staring directly at him. "I'll go." And then he turned on his heel and started walking.

She stood in sea foam, watching him stride away from her across the sand.

That day, Dante did something he'd never done before, something of which he did not in any way approve.

Though there was nothing physically wrong with him, he called in sick.

He called in sick and then he sat in the house and thought about Gracie. When he started to feel like the walls were closing in, he took a beer out on the deck. He sat at the table, with Owen moping at his feet, and thought about Gracie some more.

The next day, he called in again.

That day, he did exactly what he'd done the day before. It was just him and Owen, in the house or on the deck. He stared into space with Gracie on his mind.

Saturday, he was just about to call in a third time when he somehow managed to stop himself in the act of picking up his phone.

He still had *some* self-respect, after all, a little kernel of it, deep inside. He had C Watch that night and damn it, when the time came, he was going to work.

It started raining at around ten that morning, a drizzly, gray, lackluster kind of rain. He stood at the slider and watched it dribble down from the sky and wondered what was wrong with him, really.

Something definitely was. Gracie had said she loved him and he'd said thank you and walked away.

The more he thought about that, the more he despised himself.

He'd always considered himself a good man, one who did the right thing, a guy who stepped up when action was called for, did his part no matter how tough the challenge. Not some tongue-tied idiot who turned and ran the minute shit got real.

This was so bad.

He missed Gracie so much. He couldn't stop thinking of her, of her big heart and smart mouth, of the way she'd stood there so proudly and said it right out loud: *Dante, I'm in love with you.*

It was driving him crazy. *She* was driving him crazy. He'd never felt this way before.

Yeah, it had been hard when Marjorie left. He'd missed her and the girls. He'd regretted that he'd failed so miserably at his marriage, been ashamed that he hadn't been able to make it work. But that had been nothing compared to this. He felt like Gracie had ripped his heart out, stuffed it in a suitcase and hauled it off along with her when she went.

When Marjorie left, he'd had no urge to break things.

Now? Oh, he did have that urge and it was powerful—to start grabbing random objects and throwing them at the nearest wall. The big ceramic bowl on the coffee table, for instance. It would make a very satisfying crash that would send shards flying everywhere if he hurled it at, say, the fireplace…

He was sitting on the sofa, staring at that bowl, reminding himself that breaking stuff was juvenile, messy and completely pointless, when the doorbell rang.

"Go away," he muttered to whoever was out there and continued glaring at the bowl.

The doorbell rang again. And then there was knocking.

It gave Dante a certain dark satisfaction to just sit there and contemplate that bowl.

Whoever it was went away—or so he thought until he heard knocking on the slider. Resigned, he glanced over his shoulder to see who it was: Connor, with a what-is-your-problem expression on his face. Owen was already over there, whining hopefully at the door.

Dante didn't want to talk to Connor. Or to anyone, for that matter.

But Connor had that look, the one that said he wasn't going anywhere and Dante might as well give up and open the damn door.

He dragged himself upright and went to the slider. "Yeah?" he demanded through the glass.

Connor just waited, with the rain dripping down on him.

Dante pulled the damn door open. "What's this about?"

"Let me in. We need to talk."

"What about?"

"Stop being an idiot or I'll be forced to beat some sense into you. God knows you probably deserve it."

Apprehension clutched at his gut and tightened the skin at the back of his neck. "Is Gracie okay?"

"She's fine—no thanks to you. And it's wet out here." Connor stepped forward.

Dante cleared the doorway and let him pass. "You want coffee?"

"Is it made?" Connor raked his damp hair back, swiping raindrops off his forehead in the process.

"Only takes a minute."

"Sure, whatever." Connor pulled out a chair at the table and Dante went over and brewed him a cup.

Neither of them said a word until Dante set a full mug in front of Connor and took the chair across from him.

Then Connor commanded, "Talk."

Dante eyed him warily. "There is no point in—"

"Talk."

A stare down ensued.

Dante dropped his gaze first. "How much do you know?"

Connor rubbed at the space between his eyes, like maybe Dante was giving him a headache or something. "She called Liam Monday." Liam was fourth-born in the Bravo family, a year younger than Connor. "She asked if she could borrow a truck the next day. So, Tuesday, while you were at work apparently, Liam, Harper and Hailey helped her pack up her stuff and haul it all to the cottage.

"Tuesday night, Liam called me. He explained about moving Gracie to the cottage and asked what was going on. He said it was obvious she was wrecked about something, but she wouldn't say squat about it and Hailey and Harper wouldn't talk, either. So last night, I stopped by the Sea Breeze for a beer on the way home from work—or that was the pretense, anyway. Really, I just wanted to check on Gracie, see how she was doing. She wouldn't tell me anything, either. But I'm guessing you broke my beautiful, sweet baby sister's heart and so here I am to find out what is the matter with you." He knocked back a slug of caffeine and set down the mug. "I'll say it again. Talk."

"There's nothing to say."

Connor was absorbed in an intense study of his coffee mug. "Talk."

"I'm not…what she needs. And she left. And now it's just me and the dog and both of us are miserable."

"But you sent her away, right?"

"I didn't. No. She left. She left because there were things she wanted that I couldn't give her."

"Couldn't? Or wouldn't?"

"Fine. Wouldn't. Happy now?"

"Not about this. Why?" Connor demanded.

"Why what?"

Connor shot him a glance of pure exasperation. "If you're not willing to give my sister what she needs, why are you miserable that she left?"

Dante shook his head. "There is no point in talking about this."

"Answer the question."

"Because I feel empty. I'm lonely, I'm sad and I hate it."

"You hate what?"

"Being here without her. It's bad, okay. It's no good at all. I mean, I just don't get this. I hate this. I've got all these damn *feelings* and I don't know what to do with them."

"Yeah, well. It's never a great idea to throw away what you want the most."

"I did not throw Gracie away."

"Yeah, Dante. You kind of did."

"You don't get it."

"Well, one of us is clueless. And it's not me. Dante, we've been best friends on and off for as long as I can remember. I know you better than you think. You're a good man, the best. But you've got way too much pride. You think things ought to be a certain way and you don't like feeling out of control. I remember when you got together with Marjorie. She is such a nice woman. No drama, no conflict. You said she was perfect, but what you really meant was she was *safe*. She wasn't going to make you feel the way your dad's always felt about your mom, the way I feel about your sister—all hot and bothered and out of control. You really thought you'd dodged a bullet with Marjorie, didn't you?"

Dante was thinking that punching Connor in the face just might be more satisfying than throwing a bowl at the fireplace. "What exactly are you getting at?"

Connor had the balls to chuckle. "Gracie. She's not safe and she's not always going to do things your way. But she *is* the one for you."

Dante scoffed. "The *one*?"

"That's right. Now you finally know what it's like. Welcome to the real thing, Dante. Love. It's finally happened for you."

After Connor left, Dante decided to stop moping around the house. He went out and bought groceries, took Owen for a run on the beach and then headed over to the gym for an hour. He had dinner with his parents and his second-youngest brother, Marco.

And then he went to work. It was a busy Saturday night with a couple of robberies to deal with and a nasty domestic that had almost turned tragic. He had no time for brooding on whether or not true love had finally caught up with him in the form of a gorgeous blonde with a wicked sense of humor and zero willingness to put up with his crap.

Sunday, he went through the motions of living all over again. Monday was the same. The week went on like most weeks do.

It was Friday before he began to accept that he was not going to get the woman he loved by just getting up and getting through each day like some wimpy little dweeb.

A real move would have to be made.

He spent the weekend figuring out exactly what that move should be.

Monday was Gracie's first in-service day at Valentine Bay High. School was starting the day after Labor Day and that meant she had essentially one week to get her classroom student ready. At the same time, she had to attend a raft of meetings—OSHA, first aid, departmental, new-teacher orientation. Some of those meetings seemed to drag on forever. Between the meetings, there was the mad scramble to get her room in order. There was too much to do and not enough time to do it in. The upside? The work overload kept her from dwelling on how much she missed a certain stubborn, impossible man.

Love was hard. Especially when you felt torn in two—your brain telling you it just wasn't going to work out while your heart screamed to hold on, never give up!

Her heart just wouldn't quit hoping. Every night since she left him, she would lie there in bed in the dark, her whole body aching, just kind of burning up from inside with the love that Dante wouldn't let her give him.

She needed to forget him.

But she knew that wasn't going to be happening anytime soon. Her job was to keep a reasonably good attitude, put one foot in front of the other and get through each day.

As she drove back to the cottage that Monday afternoon, she reminded herself that she needed to focus on the good things—on the sunshiny day after the gray, rainy weekend, on her first real job as a teacher at last.

"Good things," she whispered under her breath as she turned onto the tree-shaded driveway that led up to the cottage. "Good things…"

The cottage came into view—along with Dante's crew cab in the cleared space where she and her sisters parked their vehicles. The man himself, in dark-wash jeans and a crisp blue button-down, sat on the front step in the thick shade of the tall trees.

For a terrifying moment, she was certain she must be imagining him, that her hopeful, yearning heart had her seeing the impossible.

She blinked three times in rapid succession. He was still there, his expression a little apprehensive, so handsome that just looking at him twisted the knife of longing within her all over again.

Her frantic heart beating so loud she couldn't hear herself think, she realized she'd stopped breathing. "Breathe, now," she whispered, "just breathe," as she carefully guided her Toyota into the empty spot beside the pickup and turned off the engine.

She had stacks of stuff to carry in, but her hands were shaking and her body felt strangely numb. If she tried to carry her big tote and her laptop and the ream and a half of paperwork, it would probably all end up on the ground.

So, then. Later for that.

With slow deliberation, she pushed open her door and swung her rubbery legs to the ground. They wobbled a little when she stood, but it was okay. She could do this.

Dante was already on his feet. She started toward him, her eyes tracking right and left—anywhere but directly at him.

Which was cowardly. Weak.

And she was not weak.

She needed to face him, to look directly at him. Whatever she saw when she looked in his eyes would tell her everything. Maybe more than she wanted to know.

A certain calm descended.

She paused in midstep and made herself meet his eyes.

That was all it took. Just one look in those dark, hungry eyes of his.

One look, and she knew.

"Gracie." He said her name like it was everything to him, like *she* was everything.

She took three more steps and stopped maybe two feet away from him. He reached for her hand. She gave it.

Oh, that moment. She would hold it in her heart for all of her life. The moment his strong fingers wrapped around hers, the first time he touched her after she knew that he had figured it out.

He finally understood. She was his and he was hers and that was how it was going to be. Now. Tomorrow. For all the days to come.

"It's nice out here," she said, and realized her

knees were kind of wobbly all over again. "Can we sit down?"

"Sure." Keeping a firm grip on her hand, he dropped back to the step. She sat down beside him.

A lovely sense of unreality assailed her. Was this actually happening?

Fear crept in.

Did she have it all wrong? Had she totally misread the promise she'd seen in his eyes?

There was a simple way to find out.

She straightened her shoulders and made herself ask him, "So then, next Sunday? Dinner with the Bravo family up at Daniel's house?"

He leaned in until there was barely an inch between his lips and hers. "God, yes." He said it prayerfully, a sacred trust between the two of them. "I'm in."

A bolt of pure joy blasted through her. This was real. It was happening. She let out the breath she hadn't realized she was holding. "I'm so glad."

His dark gaze scanned her face slowly. With something like reverence. "I love you, Gracie. So much. All my life I've been scared of loving someone the way I love you."

She couldn't help grinning. "You're still scared."

He stared at her, his gaze steady and true. "I'll get over it. As long as you're here to help me deal with all these big emotions you somehow make me feel."

"Big emotions are good," she informed him gently. "You're going to learn to love them."

He made a low sound. It might have been agreement. With maybe just a hint of irony, too. "As long as you're with me."

"I will be. Right here beside you, no matter what. I swear it."

He closed the sliver of distance between them. Their lips met, careful. Hesitant.

At first.

And then his arms came around her. She breathed in his beloved scent of cedar and spice as they shared a kiss full of promises she knew now they were both going to keep.

A cool wind came up, stirring the trees, creating a space between the branches so the late-afternoon sun could reach them. It felt good, the breeze, the brief warmth of sunlight on her upturned face.

She opened her eyes. They shared a long glance of perfect understanding. He wrapped an arm around her and she rested her head on his shoulder.

For the longest time, they sat without speaking, just being there on the front step under the wind-ruffled trees, together.

And then he took her hand again. She straightened enough to meet his waiting eyes.

"Marry me," he said. Before she could answer, he went on, "Don't decide now. I just want you to think about it. Think about it knowing that I want to spend the rest of my life with you and whatever it takes to get there, well, that's what I'm willing to do and…" His voice trailed off. He looked terrified, suddenly. "I'm pushing too fast."

She squeezed his hand. "No, you're not."

"You sure?"

"I am. It's what I want, too. Marriage. To you, Dante. And I just might be getting that urge to do something crazy like drag you to the courthouse right now, today."

"Something crazy sounds pretty damn good to me."

"Except…"

"Except what?" he demanded gruffly.

"I'm thinking we really need to consider how Nicole and Natalie are going to feel before we go taking any major steps."

"They love you almost as much as I do."

"I love them, too. And for their sake, we can't rush things. They need time to adjust. Up till now, they've had you all to themselves. We have to show them that my being in the picture won't threaten what they have with you."

He turned her hand over, spread it open and brought her palm to his warm lips for a sweet, quick brush of a kiss. "Go on."

"I think first, Nic and Nat need to start seeing us as a couple."

"Yeah. I get that."

"They're coming to you this weekend, right?"

"Right."

"Okay, so I want to move back to the cabin before they get here. That's going to be a challenge for me. I've got a full week of meetings and classroom prep at the high school."

His thick eyebrows were suddenly scrunching together. "The moving's no problem. I'll make it happen."

"Then why are you frowning?"

"I was just thinking that what I really want is for you to move into the main house with me."

"Oh, Dante." She pressed her hand to his smooth-shaven cheek. "I want that, too."

"Well, then, why don't you just—"

She silenced him with a finger to his soft lips. "We'll get there. But for the girls' sake, I think we need to start from where we were when they came back two weeks ago. Our mission this visit is to get them to begin seeing us as a couple, while at the same time reassuring them that they are still your priority, that you're no less theirs than you ever were. That you're just…starting to be mine, too."

"Our mission," he said in dazed voice. "We have a damn mission?"

She laughed at his bewilderment. "Yes, we have a mission. And it begins with me at the cabin, everything pretty much as it was when they left two weeks ago, only this visit, we introduce a little hand-holding and some mild PDAs. See how they take it. And then at some point, you have the talk with them, explain to them that we're, um, dating."

"Dating? We're getting married, that's way beyond dating."

She tugged his hand up and over her shoulder so his arm was wrapped around her again. "It might take time, to get Natalie and Nicole comfortable with the idea that we're a couple."

He drew her in closer and dropped a kiss on the top of her head. "Okay, so I'll try to be patient. We'll see how it goes."

"Good." She tipped her head back to look at him, happiness moving through her, filling her up with all the possibilities that came with giving her heart to the right man and knowing that they had their own forever ahead of them. "One way or another, it's all going to work out."

He kissed the end of her nose. "Promise?"

"Yes, Dante." She reached up to clasp the back of his neck and pulled him down for a kiss. "I do."

Epilogue

A little while later, she led him into the cottage and down the hall to her room. She closed the door and engaged the privacy lock so they could share a more intimate celebration of their reunion.

When her sisters got home, Grace explained that she was moving back to the cabin at Dante's place.

Harper asked, "Should we be celebrating?"

Dante hooked his arm around Grace and pulled her close. "She said yes."

Hailey clapped her hands at the news.

Harper grinned. "Congratulations. You're a very lucky man."

Grace warned, "Keep it to yourselves for now.

We need to see how Nicole and Natalie feel about the situation."

Hailey vowed, "We won't tell a soul."

Harper had a bottle of prosecco in the back of the fridge. She popped the cork and they shared a toast to love and happiness. Then Grace packed a bag and followed Dante to his house.

Owen's glum mood vanished the minute Gracie walked in the door. She greeted him with hugs and enthusiastic reassurances that she was home to stay.

The next day, Dante got all of Gracie's stuff moved back to the cabin. Even with her demanding schedule at the high school, she managed to get everything put away before the girls arrived.

On Saturday morning, Dante insisted that Grace go with him to the pickup spot. The second Roger's white minivan rolled to a stop, the girls jumped out and ran back to the crew cab as Grace and Dante got out to greet them. Nobody seemed the least surprised to see her there. Not Nat or Nic—or Marjorie or Roger.

There was a barbecue at the Santangelo grand-parents' house that afternoon. Dante invited Grace and she said she would love to come. Dante's mom, Catriona, hugged Grace at the door and then wore a giant smile on her face all through dinner.

As for the girls, they didn't say a word that day

or Sunday about what might be going on between their dad and Gracie. Not even when the four of them went to the Bravo house for Sunday dinner.

But then on Monday morning, Grace woke to a knock on the cabin door. She could hear the twins out there, giggling and chattering together.

She rolled out of bed and went to let them in. "Am I invited for breakfast?"

"Yes!" declared Natalie.

Nic gazed up at her with a strange expression on her face—a little shy, kind of coy. "Gracie?"

"Hmm?"

Nic's cheeks flushed the prettiest shade of red as Nat asked the question for her in a nervous little whisper. "Are you our dad's girlfriend?"

She'd imagined Dante discussing this subject with them first. But it was a direct question, so she answered honestly. "I am, yes." And before she could decide the right thing to say next, the girls started squealing in delight.

The three of them danced around the cabin, laughing and hugging. Then at breakfast, Nicole announced, "We're too old to be flower girls. So when you guys get married, can we be your bridesmaids?"

So much for taking it slow with the girls. Across the table, Dante looked a bit smug. After all, he'd told her the girls would be thrilled to see them together. She nodded at Nat and then at Nic and said she would be honored to have them as her bridesmaids.

Several hours later, at the drop-off point, the twins ran straight to Roger's minivan to inform their mother and stepfather that their dad was going to marry Gracie—and they would be bridesmaids.

Both Marjorie and Roger seemed to take the news in stride. It was almost as if they already knew that something was going on between Marjorie's ex and Grace.

That night, and for every night thereafter, Grace slept in Dante's bed.

In mid-October, he took her out to find the right ring. She chose a diamond solitaire on a platinum band.

And on the second Saturday of the following June, Gracie walked down the aisle to him. When the pastor said he could kiss his bride, Dante lifted her veil gently, reverently. He gathered her into his arms and whispered, "Forever," as he covered her eager mouth with his.

* * * * *

*Watch for Hailey's story
coming in October 2020,
only from Harlequin Special Edition.*

#2767 THE TEXAN'S BABY BOMBSHELL

The Fortunes of Texas: Rambling Rose • by Allison Leigh

When Laurel Hudson is found—alive but with amnesia—no one is more relieved than Adam Fortune. He will do whatever it takes to reunite mother and son, even if it means a road trip in extremely close quarters. Will the long journey home remind Laurel how much they truly share?

#2768 COMING TO A CROSSROADS

Matchmaking Mamas • by Marie Ferrarella

When the Matchmaking Mamas recommend Dr. Ethan O'Neil as a potential ride-share customer to Liz Bellamy, it's a win-win financial situation. Yet the handsome doctor isn't her usual fare. Kind, witty and emotionally guarded, Ethan thinks love walked out years ago, until his unlikely connection with his beautiful, hardworking chauffeur.

#2769 THEIR NINE-MONTH SURPRISE

Sutter Creek, Montana • by Laurel Greer

Returning from vacation, veterinary tech Lachlan Reid is shocked—the woman he's been dreaming about for months is on his doorstep, pregnant. Lachlan has always wanted to be a dad and works tirelessly to make Marisol see his commitment. But can he convince marriage-shy Marisol to form the family of their dreams?

#2770 HER SAVANNAH SURPRISE

The Savannah Sisters • by Nancy Robards Thompson

Kate Clark's Vegas wedding trip wasn't for *her* wedding. But she still got a husband! Aidan Quindlin broke her heart in high school. And if she's not careful, the tempting single dad could do it again. Annulment is the only way to protect herself. Then she learns she's pregnant...

#2771 THE SECRET BETWEEN THEM

The Culhanes of Cedar River • by Helen Lacey

After months of nursing her father back to health, artist Leah Culhane is finally focusing on her work again. But her longtime crush on Sean O'Sullivan is hard to forget. Sean has come home but is clearly keeping secrets from everyone, even his family. So why does he find himself wanting to bare his soul—and his heart—to Leah?

#2772 THE COWBOY'S CLAIM

Tillbridge Stables • by Nina Crespo

Chloe Daniels is determined to land the role of a lifetime. Even if she's terrified to get on a horse! And the last thing her reluctant teacher, Tristan Tillbridge, wants is to entertain a pampered actress. But the enigmatic cowboy soon discovers that Chloe's as genuine as she is gorgeous. Will this unlikely pair discover that the sparks between them are anything but an act?

SPECIAL EXCERPT FROM

◆ HARLEQUIN
SPECIAL EDITION

*When Laurel Hudson is found—alive but with
amnesia—no one is more relieved than Adam Fortune.
He will do whatever it takes to reunite mother and son,
even if it means a road trip in extremely close quarters.
Will the long journey home remind Laurel how much
they truly share?*

*Read on for a sneak preview of the final book in
The Fortunes of Texas: Rambling Rose continuity,*
The Texan's Baby Bombshell *by Allison Leigh.*

He'd been falling for her from the very beginning. But
that kiss had sealed the deal for him.

Now that glossy oak-barrel hair slid over her shoulder
as Laurel's head turned and she looked his way.

His step faltered.

Her eyes were the same stunning shade of blue they'd
always been. Her perfectly heart-shaped face was pale
and delicate looking even without the pink scar on her
forehead between her eyebrows.

Her eyebrows pulled together as their eyes met.

Remember me.

Remember us.

The words—unwanted and unexpected—pulsed
through him, drowning out the splitting headache and the
aching back and the impatience, the relief and the pain.

Then she blinked those incredible eyes of hers and he realized there was a flush on her cheeks and she was chewing at the corner of her lips. In contrast to her delicate features, her lips were just as full and pouty as they'd always been.

Kissing them had been an adventure in and of itself.

He pushed the pointless memory out of his head and then had to shove his hands in the pockets of his jeans because they were actually shaking.

"Hi." Puny first word to say to the woman who'd made a wreck out of him.

Still seated, she looked up at him. "Hi." She sounded breathless. "It's…it's Adam, right?"

The pain sitting in the pit of his stomach then had nothing to do with anything except her. He yanked his right hand from his pocket and held it out. "Adam Fortune."

She looked uncertain, then slowly settled her hand into his.

Unlike Dr. Granger's firm, brief clasp, Laurel's touch felt chilled and tentative. And it lingered. "I'm Lisa."

God help him. He was not strong enough for this.

Don't miss
The Texan's Baby Bombshell *by Allison Leigh,*
available June 2020 wherever
Harlequin Special Edition books and ebooks are sold.

Harlequin.com

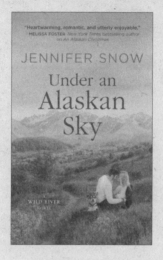